ROOM 207

MARNELLE TOKIO

ILLUSTRATED BY LINDA HENDRY

Text copyright © 2006 by Marnelle Tokio
Illustrations copyright © 2006 by Linda Hendry

Published in Canada by Tundra Books,
75 Sherbourne Street, Toronto, Ontario M5A 2P9

Published in the United States by Tundra Books of Northern New York,
P.O. Box 1030, Plattsburgh, New York 12901

Library of Congress Control Number: 2005927013

Library and Archives Canada Cataloguing in Publication

Tokio, Marnelle
    Room 207 / Marnelle Tokio ; illustrated by Linda Hendry.

ISBN 10: 0-88776-695-1
ISBN 13: 978-0-88776-695-4

    I. Hendry, Linda   II. Title.   III. Title: Room two hundred seven.

PS8589.O639R66 2006   jC813'.6   C2005-904078-5

ONTARIO ARTS COUNCIL
CONSEIL DES ARTS DE L'ONTARIO

We acknowledge the financial support of the Government of Canada
through the Book Publishing Industry Development Program (BPIDP)
and that of the Government of Ontario through the Ontario Media
Development Corporation's Ontario Book Initiative.
We further acknowledge the support of the Canada Council for the Arts
and the Ontario Arts Council for our publishing program.

Design: Terri Nimmo   Cover Concept Design: Isabeau Tokio Welter

Printed in Canada

1 2 3 4 5 6   10 09 08 07 06 05

This book is for the real ROOM 207. Not the concrete walls, or the too-small cubbies, or the rug that was fun to pick at. I mean the people who made ROOM 207 real for me. You know who you are. But if you don't mind, I'd like to tell the world.

Thank you and asante to Ali, Adrian, Andrea, Aliya, and Araf. Mahalo, very much mahalo to Beau. Cheers to Cherise, Christina, and Christopher. Danke to Derek, Di, and Dorijan. Faleminderit to Forrest. Hvala to Hiwot. Iuspagara to Isaiah. Juspaxar to Jasper, Jona, and Jordan. Kiitos to Kunhee. Laengz zingh to Latifah and Leon. Merci beaucoup to Malcolm, Maria, and Michelle. Na gode to Nishat, Nicholas, and Nicolas without an "h" but a place in my heart. Puorra bebe la to Peter. Rahmat to Romans. Spasibo to Sorna and Sunjin. And an Aussie "ta" to Tirth.

For you as well, Lynne Timney. No matter where we came from, you made us feel at home in your class. You are the hands-down-best teacher ever. And for Sibylle who lent me her name and has dedicated hundreds of volunteer hours to Room 207, not to mention a million mints.

CONTENTS

CAST OF CHARACTERS

THE KIDS

Samantha Napps

The Gumtree Twins (Todd & Adam)

Pugh

Rodan Avitar

Miles Marsbar

Nina Zallina & Olive Calmatta

Erik Erikson

Juliet Faintheart

Jose Xavier

Brittany Madison / Heather Wales

THE ADULTS

Mr. Bellows (Principal)

Nurse Payne

Miss Chimney

THE CLASS PETS...

Butterbum   Professor Shrimpington

Pourquoi

Amadeus (the ghost cat)

HOOLEY-DOOLEY

Samantha had stayed up till 3:00 in the morning watching *Night Of The Living Dead*. She walked like a zombie through the gate and onto the playground of Anna Swan Heights Elementary. Even after a whole summer of practicing, Samantha was still not a morning person. She wore her back-to-school backpack on her front and was combing her hair with a strip of bacon. She yawned. A beetle flew into her mouth. "Mommm nooo," she muttered, "no more Crunchy Pops."

Pugh was standing by the double doors when he saw Samantha down the bug. He swallowed hard and turned the same gray-green as his T-shirt. "So much for the most important meal of the day." He quickly moved to the kindergarten bench where the little kids kept their sand buckets.

Todd sat cross-legged underneath the basketball net, heading balls back to the kids who scored. He had already eaten his lunch and was thinking out loud about dinner, "Mmm, bangers and mash would be good."

Todd Gumtree and his twin brother, Adam, had just moved from Australia. The Seal Breath Circus had recruited their parents because they trained waltzing walruses, all named Mark. Mr. and Mrs. Gumtree traveled a lot so they had pulled Granny out from under Ayers Rock and made her move with them to look after the boys. Granny fed the boys thirteen times a day. Adam was glad to start school, play something other than Crazy Eights, and maybe wear off all that food. He stared at the tetherball rope and pole, "Ay Todders!" He threw a pebble at his twin to get his attention. "Why do ya think they call it *tether*ball if they don't bother to tie the ball up?"

Rodan squatted under the monkey bars and peered at an oil slick in a puddle. He stirred it with a stick to make a jagged rainbow. "This came from dead dinosaurs," he called up to Miles.

Miles was reading *Jurassic Park* at the top of the slide.

Nina was hugging everyone. Even the boys.

Olive grouched at everyone. Especially the boys.

Erik collected lunch money from the little kids. He wouldn't accept checks. "Cash and cookies only," he demanded, sneering into small faces.

Mr. Bellows, the principal, grabbed Erik by the ear and made him give the money back. Then he gave Erik the first detention of the new school year.

The rest of the kids were having a good time. They ran too fast. They threw balls too hard. Some found sharp sticks and others almost lost their eyes. The usual suspects tattled, told secrets and lies, or joked about the stupid things they had done over summer.

Anna Swan Heights Elementary

The sun was shining on the perfect first day of school.

Mr. Bellows stood beaming in the middle of the play-ground. He cleared his throat to make a big announcement. "May I have your attention please?"

Nobody paid him any attention.

Mr. Bellows turned red, which was unusual because he usually turned purple. He was short and round and yelled a lot. The kids called him Blueberry Bellows, but not to his face or his back or out loud. They called him Blueberry Bellows in a whisper.

Mr. Bellows coughed in an elephant-getting-a-peanut-shell-out-of-his-throat kind of way. "Excuse me people!" he trumpeted.

A kindergarten kid whizzed by on a tricycle. "Why? Did you burp, mister?"

"What!" Mr. Bellows shook his purple head. "No, I . . . EVERYONE FREEZE OR YOU WILL BE PUT BACK A GRADE – STARTING TODAY," he bellowed.

Every girl, every boy, and even the yard monitors froze to the point of frostbite.

"Thank you!" Mr. Bellows said, and held up two fingers. "Two announcements." He changed to one finger, "Firstly, I would like you all to welcome our new kindergarten teacher, *and my niece*, Miss Weedwhacker."

A woman with a permanent dolphin smile waved like the queen. She had eyes like a lizard.

Bellows lowered his hand. "Lovely isn't she?" He grinned with pride, "I would like to announce that we're going to do the Best Classroom Contest a little differently this year. I will be observing all classes for the first three weeks of school instead of the last three to determine which group of students, *and their leaders*, are worthy of the greatest prize that has ever been offered in the history of Anna Swan Heights. First prize is so magnificent that we will not be awarding second and third prizes as they would look so embarrassingly puny by comparison." Mr. Bellows paused for dramatic effect, not because he had run out of air. In fact, he had so much air that there wasn't any left for the kids. They didn't need it. They were holding their breaths.

"Does anyone want to know what first prize is?" whispered Mr. Bellows.

"YES!"

"The winners of this year's Best Classroom Contest," Mr. Bellows did a drum roll on his big belly, "will spend seven days tasting and creating twenty-three new flavors of ice cream at the Dream Cream Factory right here in our town of Tatamagouche!"

The playground unfroze. Noise erupted like lava from a volcano.

Todd grabbed Adam by the shoulders and shook him until he looked like a bobblehead in a blender.

"Hooley-dooley, mate! All-you-can-eat ice lollies for a week!"

"UNFAIR!" screamed Brittany Madison Heather Wales who was standing beside the twins. "TO-TALLY UNFAIR!" she marched up to Mr. Bellows and tugged on his vest.

"Yes Britty?" asked Principal Bellows, distracted by the noise.

Brittany Madison Heather Wales lifted her foot to stomp on Mr. Bellows' toe. She stomped on the toes of people who didn't use all four of her names when addressing her. And she always used the word "addressing." "Are you *addressing* me?" she demanded.

"Ah, yes. . . ." Mr. Bellows leaned down and focused on the girl's face. "Yes, of course, Brittany Madison Heather Wales," he smiled. "How is your father's fundraising for a school pool coming along?"

"*Not good* . . . if I don't win the Best Classroom Contest," she glared.

"And why wouldn't you have a chance to win like everyone else?" Mr. Bellows asked, in his most soothing voice.

"Because I'm not in Miss Chimney's class!" she blasted.

Mr. Bellows looked at her blankly.

She put her hands on her hips and gave him a sticky-sweet smile. "Miss Chimney's class has won the stupid contest four years in a row **because her classroom has the big tank with a baby shark that has a feeding frenzy every Wednesday and the model tar pits with *real* tar and fake robot dinosaurs AND A THIRTY-THREE FLAVOR SLURPY MACHINE!**"

Mr. Bellows' ears were ringing. "But your parents requested that you be placed in Mrs. New's room because you've already had nine cavities from too many sweets," he replied, holding up his hands.

"BUT I CAN'T WIN IF I'M NOT IN 207!" She stomped on his big toe.

The principal winced. Brittany Madison Heather Wales went to throw a royal tantrum under the crab-apple tree where she held court every recess.

Nina jumped up, down, and sideways, "She's right, you know! Room 207 does have amazing stuff." Nina stopped suddenly. She looked over at the apple tree and frowned, "But that might not be fair to everyone."

"Her highness will get over it," Olive poked her fingers into Nina's cheeks and pushed them up into a

The Dream Cream Factory

smile. Nina started jumping again, this time flapping her arms. "Isn't Dream Cream a floating factory?"

"Yep," said Samantha. "It's the old ferry painted like a big black-and-white cow that floats around the bay."

"How much fun is *that*!" Nina squeezed her eyes shut and grinned a grin that threatened to swallow her face.

Olive and Samantha stared at her.

Nina practically exploded with excitement, "Who knows where we'll end up!"

Pugh screwed up his face, "I'm not very good at sea," he mumbled and turned as red as the lobsters his dad caught for a living.

Erik overheard Pugh and thought for once the Best Classroom Contest wasn't the lamest contest on the planet. Because anything that would get him out of schoolwork and make Pugh miserable was cool.

Mr. Bellows blew his air horn to let everyone know school had officially started.

WELCOME TO ROOM 207

The river of baseball hats and backpacks flowed through the double doors. The older kids went up the stairs like salmon swimming up stream. Some jumped ahead. Others fell behind. Teachers stood and watched at the side like bears waiting to snatch any tasty looking fish.

The summer voices of the students crashed like waves against sand-colored walls, and washed back over them, drowning out Mrs. Watson who was reading September's cafeteria menu over the PA system.

Mr. Bellows' air horn had run out of air. He marched down the middle of the hall blasting his whistle. The one that made the sound like summer never happened and no one would ever have fun again.

Everyone plugged their ears.

"Now," snapped Mr. Bellows, "can everyone hear me?"

"What?" drawled Samantha.

"Pardon?" asked Nina.

"Huh?" grunted Miles.

Mr. Bellows grabbed Miles by the wrists and pulled like one man with a wishbone. "TAKE YOUR FINGERS OUT OF YOUR EARS!" He yelled so loud that Miles' ears hurt.

Miles motioned for everyone to unplug.

"May I remind you that the words 'Ladies and Gentlemen' are not titles, but occupations and I expect all of you to be fully employed. You will conduct yourselves down the hall to your *offices* in a quiet manner. Do *not* stop in front of the workplace that suffered a most grievous accident over the holidays. You may continue your commute."

Every muscle in every body had been jumping out of its skin. Now everyone just wanted to stand still and eyeball the "most grievous accident."

The wreck of Room 207.

There were no walls. Not between the room and the hall. Not between the room and the outside. If you wanted to, you could run from your locker, across the hall, across the classroom floor, and jump into the oak tree. If you missed, you would fall two floors and land in the kindergarten sandbox.

If you could get through the slime, that is. Yellowy-green slime, whitish slime, and clear slime covered everything in the room. It looked like a huge troll with a bad cold had used the classroom as a Kleenex.

Almost nothing had survived. Body parts were strewn everywhere – arms of chairs, legs of tables, feet from desks. Sheldon the Skeleton's skull had blown off, landing in his hand. Books were stuck to the ceiling. Posters papered the floor. There was a mound of brown stuff in the corner where Miss Chimney's desk used to be. The only thing left standing was the steel door and the door jamb. It was crisscrossed with yellow caution tape that said DO NOT CROSS. DANGER ZONE.

The students of rooms 204, 205, and 206 craned their necks like giraffes to get a look as they disappeared through the doors of their own classrooms. The students of rooms 208 through 211 filed past Room 207 slow and silent as snails.

Except Brittany Madison Heather Wales. She flipped open her cell phone and yelled, "Cancel my class transfer Daddy." She stuck her tongue out as she walked by. "No slurpies for you . . . *suckers!*"

One by one the doors clicked shut leaving the students of Room 207 alone in the hall wondering what to do.

"No feeding frenzy," said Todd. His jaw dropped to the floor.

"No tar pits," said Adam scratching under his arm.

"Holy crap," said Olive.

"We don't need to start the year off with that kind of language." Miss Chimney's voice bounced down the hall. She came right behind it wearing denim and cobwebs. She walked past the children and stopped in front of the door. She reached through the yellow tape with one hand and took a hammer out of her front pocket

with the other. She pulled
the nails that held the
Room 207 nameplate to
the door and stuck them
between her clenched teeth.
Miss Chimney's rubber boots
squeaked as she did an about
face and greeted her students.
"Guht orning cass!" she said.

The new students of Room
207 stood in horror as their teacher
grinned at them with a mouth full
of shining silver nails.

DELIVERY

"**G**ood morning?" asked Miles.

Miss Chimney spat nails back into the door to make a happy face. "Yes! Too good to waste any more time standing here. Follow me."

Miles usually did what any teacher asked him to do, but this time he couldn't help himself. He ducked under the caution tape, swiped a finger full of slime and gave it a good whiff. It smelled like four things: vanilla cookies, sun screen, glue sticks, and Snuggle Wuggle fabric softener. He tucked the slime behind his ear like a glob of hair gel so Rodan could do a more thorough analysis later. Then Miles ran to catch up.

The children walked single file like ants, following the behind in front. Up the hall, down the stairs, through the playground, and across the soccer field until they

arrived at the edge of Anna Swan Heights School prop-erty in front of the original Anna Swan Heights School-house, built in 1903.

Every year they had heard that the one-room build-ing was supposed to be torn down. But it was always forgotten and left to sink a little lower in the mud and lean a little more to the right and shed all its layers of paint like a tree drops leaves in fall.

It stood before them bare and gray.

But it had walls. And no tape on the door. Miss Chimney marched up to the door and nailed what she had taken from the school. Then she swung back the door, stepped inside and said, "Welcome to Room 207."

Creak . . . creak . . . creak . . . The floorboards pro-
tested as the children entered their new old classroom.
Wooden desks with attached worn seats had lift-up lids
and were set in rows facing the big black chalkboard.
ROOM 207 GRADE 5 was written in fluorescent orange
chalk. A piano with keys that looked like old yellow
teeth was jammed into the corner beside the blackboard. The walls were striped with cracks that let the
sun shine through. Century-old particles floating in
the air made the light look almost solid. The small
windows had wonky glass that warped everything like
funhouse mirrors.

Olive made a face as she looked around. "This place
is ancient," she said. "And what's with the weird little
windows?"

Nina giggled. "I think they're neat. They make the
trees look like they're belly-dancing."

Rodan gaped at the room. "Is this some kind of
human experiment?"

"Of course not," replied Miss Chimney. She headed
to the blackboard. "Why do you ask?"

"Computers . . ." Rodan lifted the lid of a desk to see
if they were built in. "There *aren't* any!"

"Excellent observation!" Miss Chimney clapped.
"That's because there is *no electricity.*"

No Internet. Rodan wanted to die. He let go of the only desktop he was going to see in Room 207. It creaked shut like a coffin lid.

"That reminds me," Miss Chimney said briskly, "sit, sit, sit. Warm up those desks. Take any one you like." She started tugging at her desk drawer. She pulled so hard the desk inched across the raised platform on which it stood. "Darn drawer won't open!" she said through clenched teeth. "You two," she said, nodding at Todd and Adam, "please come here and each hold a corner."

"Right-oh!" the boys said and grabbed hold.

Miss Chimney spit into each palm, rubbed her hands together, and wiped her hands on her overalls, then curled her fingers around the drawer handle. She put one foot against the frame and pulled again, this time with a grunt. The drawer squeaked back. "Just . . . a . . . little . . . more. . . ." Miss Chimney said, turning violet from the effort. It still wouldn't budge. Carefully she placed her other foot up against the desk. Pushing with two feet and pulling with two hands, she stuck out from her desk like a mountain climber on the face of a cliff.

Todd and Adam were having a hard time holding the desk steady. They heard a low growl like the one Granny's cat, Ralph, made on bath day. Adam's eyes widened. "Maybe the drawer doesn't want to come out. Seems it's holdin' on for its life."

Miss Chimney heaved again. The drawer let go. Miss Chimney did a backward somersault off the platform and landed on her feet in front of the chalkboard.

The things the drawer had wanted to hang onto so badly were scattered across the floor.

Miss Chimney eyed the mess like a hawk and found her prey. "Ah there you are," she cried, picking up what looked like a tiny teakettle with a trigger, "I went over my *you-know-what* for you." She shook her finger at it.

The students stared at their teacher.

Miss Chimney looked up. "Hasn't anybody ever seen an oilcan before?"

Nobody answered.

"You're probably wondering what we might use this for," she said, handing the can to Pugh who was sitting in the front row. "I won't keep you in suspense. I would like each of you to oil the hinges on your desks so you can lift the tops without making a sound while I'm calling roll."

Todd studied the attendance sheet on the teachers' desk. "Not much of a roster. Barely enough for two ice hockey teams and not enough for one footie!" Todd was disappointed. Adam passed Miss Chimney a pen and her clipboard.

"It's not called footie here, Todd. It's soccer," Adam told him.

"Whatever. We're still weak more than a couple of kickers!"

Miss Chimney cleared her throat, "Thank you, boys, for bringing up my next point." She waved at them to take their seats. "We are not weak. We are eleven strong as a class. As you can see this is a small room and we had to adjust the class size to fit. Other teachers had to take on extra students, so their rooms are crowded. We're very lucky to have space around us to think, to imagine, and to create." She flung her arms wide.

"I wanted to create a *soccer* team," Todd pouted and slouched in his seat.

"Well let's see who might come to your try-outs . . . Rodan Avitar?" called Miss Chimney.

"Present," answered Rodan from one of the back desks as he cleared the shelf beside him for his science samples.

"Olive Calmatta?"

"Here. Just here." Olive rolled her eyes.

"Juliet Faintheart?" asked Miss Chimney. "Is that your last name dear or a medical condition?"

"A family curse," Juliet said and smiled weakly.

"Adam Gumtree?"

"Here . . . this place feels like it could be ripe with a ghost!" whispered Adam as he moved his desk closer to his brother's.

"Todd Gumtree?"

"Here! Maybe someone put a curse on it," Todd whispered back, eyes wide.

"Miles Marsbar?"

"Here!" Miles said and pointed to an old frayed rope dangling from the rafter.

"Pugh? Is that how you pronounce your name?"

"Yes, Miss Chimney. Just like church pew," Pugh answered.

"Or what you say when your dog farts!" Olive growled.

Pugh eyed Olive nervously. "Do I have to stay in this room?" he asked.

"You could sit in the office with Olive," Miss Chimney replied and glared at Olive.

"No thank you. I'd rather be HERE," said Pugh.

"Samantha Napps . . . Samantha?"

Samantha was asleep, oiling her desk with drool. She answered with a snore.

"Brittany Madison Heather Wales?"

There was no answer.

Miss Chimney looked up from her clipboard. "No? Okay then." She put a mark on the attendance sheet.

"Nina Zallina?"

Nina jumped up and rushed over to hug Miss Chimney.

"Thanks, I needed that," Miss Chimney said and hugged her back.

Nina sat down, feeling warm and fuzzy.

Miss Chimney walked toward a boy sitting in the front row, "Everyone, I'd like to introduce our new exchange student from Mexico. This is José Xavier."

"Hola!" said José Xavier and waved as if he were in a parade.

There was a knock at the door.

"Yes? Come in," said Miss Chimney.

The door opened with a groan. Nina Zallina jumped up to oil the hinges. She tripped on a loose floorboard and flew into the only three people at Anna Swan Heights School she had never hugged: Mr. Bellows, the principal, Erik Erikson, the bully, and Nurse Payne, the school nurse.

"I'm sorry, I'm sorry." Nina scrambled to get off the pile of people.

Miss Chimney rescued Nina. Then she heaved Nurse Payne to her feet and brushed her off. Nurse Payne grabbed Erik by the shoulder and straightened him out. Then Miss Chimney and Nurse Payne squatted down behind Mr. Bellows, put their arms as far as they would go around his waist, and hauled him up.

Room 207 clapped.

Samantha woke up. "What do you think Blueberry Bellows is doing here?" she whispered.

"Making a delivery," Miles said and pointed at Erik.

PROBLEMOS

E rik stood in the doorway with his arms crossed, his feet planted, and his baseball cap on backwards. He surveyed his new domain. "How am I supposed to win Best Classroom in this *dump* . . ." his eyes came to rest on Rodan, ". . . with *these* losers."

Mr. Bellows patted Erik's shoulder. "Oh, there is no need to worry about that. In fairness to Miss Chimney and her unbroken record in the Best Classroom Contest, we believe her current classroom situation should make Room 207 exempt from the competition."

"What do ya mean *current classroom situation?*" Todd stood up, wearing his too-small desk around his too-pudgy middle like a lifesaving ring. "We get the boot 'cause our room's a bit dodgy?"

Everyone leaned toward Mr. Bellows.

"Well . . . yes." The principal turned lavender. "Each class is judged on the cleanliness and decoration of its room." He poked at a pile of mouse turds with his foot and tapped the rusty horseshoe that hung on the wall. It flipped, crashed to the floor, bounced once, and knocked him in the shin, "SHI . . . SUGAR!" he yelled, rubbing his dented leg. "Of course, student behavior is considered," he added, eyeing Erik, "and the ability to perform together." He bumped into Miss Chimney and sent her sprawling into her chair. The principal finally pirouetted to a halt in front of Todd, who was still standing with his desk stuck around his middle. "You see," he panted in Todd's face, "with only a few students in your class, it really isn't fair to you either."

Todd and his desk sat down – hard.

Mr. Bellows seemed in a hurry to leave. "Miss Chimney, it has also been decided that Miss Wales will be in Mrs. New's class and Mr. Erikson here will be joining you in your . . . uh, classroom."

Room 207 reacted with a massive groan. Nobody knew which was worse, losing the contest or gaining Erik.

The principal looked up at the crumbling timbers. "Ahhh, I'm sure his strengths will add new heights to your education."

Miles dropped his pencil and whispered to Rodan, "The only things I've ever seen Erik add are his fist and some kid's face and that equaled a black eye."

"Erik, please come up to the front and take a seat beside José," said Miss Chimney.

Erik walked down the aisle and managed to hit everyone on the right side with an elbow. He took the desk he was assigned but moved it away from José.

José just smiled at Erik and said, "Hola!"

Erik glared at him. "What's your problem?"

José smiled. "I got lots of problemos," he said. "Which one you want to talk about?"

Miss Chimney stood in front of their desks. "That's enough chatting you two. And Erik, as far as your entrance goes? If this were a hockey game, you'd get two minutes for elbowing." She folded her arms in front of her chest. "There is no penalty box here, but we do have an antique dunce chair. You can sit there after school and serve detention."

Erik winked at Miss Chimney. "Already got detention with Mr. Bellows."

"Here comes the first lesson in our new class," Miss Chimney said. She waited till everyone was quiet. "What is one detention plus one detention?"

All the kids smiled and raised their hands.

Except Erik.

"Erik?" asked Miss Chimney.

"Two detentions," replied Erik.

"Very good. I'll see you at three," said Miss Chimney.

"And I'll see him at four," Mr. Bellows said, tapping his watch. "I have lots of filing for you."

Erik's face fell.

"Good thing your class is out of the contest because these detentions would count against you!" Mr. Bellows slammed the door and headed for his office.

NURSE PAYNE

F ear of detentions from Principal Bellows kept the students of Room 207 waiting silent until he looked like a black and white marble through the school windows. Then they went wild.

Erik slammed his fist down on his desk.

José dealt a doubled-fisted blow to his desk and smiled at Erik.

"Violence makes me nauseous," Pugh squeaked.

Olive huffed, "What's making me sick is Bellows throwing us out of the contest just 'cause we have a crappy classroom."

Juliet was hyperventilating. "Can . . . he . . . do . . . that?"

"It seems rather unjust," said Rodan. "There is no evidence to suggest we are unqualified." He furrowed his brow. "It's true we have no electricity, but it's still only the first day of school."

Nina looked confused, "Why is Mr. Bellows being so mean?" she wondered aloud.

Todd was too busy to comment. He was desperately trying to get free of his desk by greasing his belly with his own spit.

"I bet Mum'll call the board and roar at someone," Adam said.

"If I could just read the rules. . . ." muttered Miles.

Samantha yawned with her eyes closed. "I don't see why we can't do the contest."

Miss Chimney raised her hand for quiet. "If you really want back in. . ." she began.

"YES!" everyone shouted.

Miss Chimney smiled, ". . . then perhaps we have to get Principal Bellows and the judges to look at Room 207 differently."

Room 207 sat in deep thought.

Olive broke the silence. "Good luck," she said. "I'll bet Britty bricks-for-brains has a vote."

There were some snickers and even Miss Chimney rolled her eyes and nodded her head.

"Ahem . . . AHEM,"

Miss Chimney looked around for the irritating noise. She was blinded by a beam of light from the climbing sun, so Nurse Payne, in her bright white uniform and white nursey shoes, was difficult to see at the back of the room.

"AHHHEMMM!" ahemmed Nurse Payne.

Miss Chimney squinted and used her hand as a visor. "Oh, yes! I'm sorry, Nurse Payne, I forgot all about you. What can we do for you?"

Nurse Payne stepped forward. "I need to check the children."

All the children slid under their desks.

"For what?" asked Miss Chimney.

"Measles, mumps, scarlet fever, poison ivy, cavities, lice, and dust."

"You're checking them for dust?" Miss Chimney brushed the cobwebs from her bangs.

"Of *course*," she huffed. "If you plan to compete in the Best Classroom Contest, then you must want to win, and you can't win if your students are dusty."

Miss Chimney looked surprised, "I didn't see any dust on them." She put her hand to her chin. "They just got back from summer vacation, so I suppose they could be rusty."

Nurse Payne looked alarmed, "Major point deduction for rust," she declared. "You'd never recover in the standings. And I would have to sand the children down and return them to primary." Nurse Payne forced her sausage-like fingers into white rubber gloves and snapped them on her wrist. She narrowed her eyes at Miss Chimney. "Pray for dust."

Samantha sneezed. She was allergic to being scared.

Todd wiped the crumbs from his shirt. Crumbs were pre-dust.

Adam cleaned his ears because he heard Miss Chimney say they were expected to dust and Adam's dad always told him that after you dust, you wax.

Adam's efforts made Miles remember the stuff behind his own ear. He opened the lid of his desk a crack, scooped the goo off with his pencil, flicked it into the corner of his desk, and ducked back under it.

Nurse Payne walked up and down the aisles. She pulled the children out, one by one, and ran a finger across their noses, behind their ears, and under their armpits, which made them giggle. Then she stuffed each child back under his or her desk.

"This one has a bald spot!" Nurse Payne said as she held Miles by the collar. "Otherwise this class *seems* acceptable." Nurse Payne turned to Miss Chimney. "Next week I will check for leaks!" Nurse Payne dropped Miles into his seat, marched out, and left the door wide open.

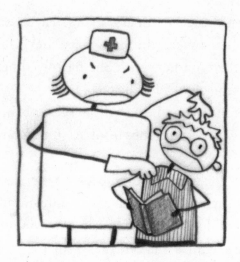

Sunlight streamed into the room. Dust swirled like smoke in the air. Dust lay on the shelves thick as a rug. But no dust was found on the children and Nurse Payne was gone. Everyone relaxed.

Miss Chimney cleared her throat, "Now that's over with," she announced. "I would like you all to meet Butterbum."

BUTTERBUM

A loud squeal came from behind Miss Chimney's desk. She reached deep into the pocket of her overalls and pulled out three carrots, tops and all. "Everyone stay very still and watch my feet," Miss Chimney ordered. She did a little tap dance, ended it by snapping off the tops of the carrots and dropping the carrots on the floor.

"*Whee wheeee WHEEEE*," squealed a little white-and-caramel-colored creature that came skittering out from under the teacher's desk. It did a homerun slide into a carrot and started to munch.

"What is that!" Juliet shrieked and climbed onto her desk.

"It's a rat, stupid!" Erik laughed.

"Rats aren't stupid," Miles said without lifting his head. He was reading *Mrs. Frisby and the Rats of Nimh*.

"Everyone here, including Butterbum, is intelligent," Miss Chimney said firmly as she bent down and picked up Butterbum. "She is a guinea pig. This summer I had a little picnic by myself in the backyard. I went into the house to get some mustard and when I came out I found her sitting in the butter."

Todd licked his lips at the thought of butter. Everyone else looked at the furball.

"Are we allowed to have pigs in school?" Juliet asked weakly as she climbed down off her desk.

Miss Chimney pulled open her bib pocket and put Butterbum inside. "Guinea pigs are rodents," she said.

"Oh," whispered Juliet.

"*This* is a pig," announced Miss Chimney, pitching the carrot tops up the aisle. "SUUEEEE!"

Slap went a mud flap that covered a hole in the wall, and a black cannonball leapt into the air and caught the carrot tops on the fly.

"Everyone, I'd like you to meet the world's second-fastest potbellied pig, Pourquoi!"

"Why. . . ." whimpered a bug-eyed Juliet.

"Exactly!" replied Miss Chimney.

"Por que?" asked José.

"Good for you!" Miss Chimney said and gave José a thumbs-up.

José gave Miss Chimney a thumbs-up right back.

Juliet shook her head, scrambled to the top of a bookcase, and fainted.

THE BIG SPIT

L unch time.

The girls left to use the bathroom in the main school building instead of the outhouse.

Erik had to stay behind to have a "chat" with Miss Chimney. They heard him yelling something about a pigsty.

"Incredible morning. Interesting classmates," Rodan commented as he walked out of the old schoolhouse with the rest of the boys.

"Yeah," said Todd, "lot's of wedgie material for that drongo Erik, but not much of a footie team for me."

"How's Erik gonna give the potbelly or piglet a wedgie?" Adam asked his brother.

"I don't know! How're they gonna kick a football?" Todd replied and shoved his brother.

"Miss Chimney didn't introduce the shrimp," said Pugh.

"What shrimp?" asked Miles.

"The one in the bowl on her desk," replied Pugh.

"Guess I was a little distracted." Miles shrugged. He looked at the rotting picnic table beside an ancient tree. "You guys want to eat here or the cafeteria?"

Pugh turned pale. "I haven't been in the cafeteria since Erik poured chocolate milk and watermelon Jell-O over my tuna sandwich and made me eat it. He called it tuna surprise. It surprised the lunch lady when I threw up all over her."

Adam's eyes got big. "You did the big spit on that hard-boiled cafeteria lady?"

Pugh kicked the dirt. "Yeah."

Adam patted Pugh on the back. "Ah, no worries mate. It served her right for dishin' out the old mystery meat."

Todd's stomach growled, "I'm starvers! Any of you blokes got some extra food?"

Rodan opened his yellow and black thermo-insulated lunch pack, which doubled as the place he kept his experiments warm or cold depending on what he was studying. He dug around and handed Miles a bag of corn chips to pass along to Todd.

Miles handed them over. "You might want to check these out for bugs first."

Todd held the bag up to the sun to see if anything but chips were making shadow puppets. "These don't have any mozzie eggs or anything in them?"

"Mosquitoes lay their eggs in water," Rodan informed him.

"Good-oh! . . . 'cause last year I had a gobble of Adam's science project. Nasty mistake. I had to lure the parasites out of my tummy by chewing on tree bark."

José came tearing out of Room 207 and grabbed the chips bag out of mid-air. "Gotcha!" he held the bag over his head in triumph. Then he saw the look in Todd's eyes. "Adios muchachos!" He punted the chips back to Todd and ran toward the playground.

"That bloke nicked my chips!" exclaimed Todd.

"Actually they were my chips," Rodan reminded him.

"That's not the point," said Todd.

Adam punched his brother on the shoulder. "Give 'im a break."

"Break! Listen," said Todd, "he can grab, he can punt …he could be a great goalie!" he yelled and ran after José.

"I guess we're not eating here," Miles said and headed with Pugh and Adam to the playground.

There were rules to the playground that everyone knew. If you were trying to catch something you would miss it. If you didn't want to get hit, something would hit you. Hard. You would do something you should never do, and that you had never done before, only when a teacher was looking right at you. But it wasn't teachers and flying things that made kids afraid of making the wrong move. It was bullies. And there was never just one bully on the playground. They usually traveled in herds. With Erik as lead bull.

Erik said he liked to spend "quality" time with other kids. Any kids that were smaller, wider, smarter, dumber, darker, lighter, brighter, sadder, or happier than he was. Back in third grade, when he first came to Anna Swan Heights, he had made an announcement: "My name is Erik. It means *one who rules*. But I'm fair. I don't discriminate. I hate everyone."

That was two years ago and he'd reigned ever since.

RODENT BOY

It wasn't until after Brittany Madison Heather Wales had gathered her fashion police and started issuing tickets that everyone opened their lunchboxes to trade the stuff someone's mom had packed for something somebody's dad had packed.

Then Erik showed up, took one bite of what he had made for himself and stuffed it in his pocket.

He walked into the middle of a seated circle of grade one kids. "Hmmm. . . ." He tickled his lips with his fingers. He picked out what he wanted as if he were choosing delicacies from a buffet. "I'll take one of these," he said, and took Fiona Appleby's perfect peach. "And this looks good." He grabbed Roger's quadruple-decker turkey and jam on waffles. Erik tucked the sandwich under his arm and took a sip of Valerie's vanilla

soymilk. "You can keep that," he snarled. He spied little Tina Totts sliding something behind her back. He slowly pulled her arm round to her front. Erik's eyes widened at the sight of the double-chocolate cupcake smothered in fudge frosting topped with a white daisy and a candy ladybug. "Oh, I really shouldn't, but I just can't help myself," he said, smiling. Then he stopped smiling.

Tina's little lower lip quivered.

"No *really*. I can't help myself. My arms are full. Follow me . . . and bring your cupcake!"

After Erik finished lunch he picked up and used the clean half of Bobby Grimbly from the kindergarten to wipe the chocolate icing off his hands. He put him in the garbage can when he was done and headed across the playground for the tetherball where Rodan was playing Todd.

Todd stood a whole Shaquille O'Neal shoe size taller than Rodan, but Rodan was winning. Rodan always won. He was good at two things. Tetherball and science. Rodan said the answer to tetherball was science plus sweat, physics and physical. Rodan's nickname was Lab Rat.

Rodan didn't notice Erik, who butted two kids standing in line. They moved. Everyone in line moved until Erik was at the front of the line. He grabbed the tetherball out of mid-air as Rodan was trying to hit the ball super hard, but the ball never came. And science dictates that bodies in motion stay in motion even if they are heading for the pavement. Then they stop. Rodan crashed to the pavement.

Erik looked down at Rodan and said, "What's the matter with you, Rodent Boy?"

Rodan blinked.

"I don't speak blinky-blinky," Eric said sarcastically. "Is that rat language? Can't you talk human, like every-one else here?" Erik turned to face the crowd.

Rodan looked at everyone as they shrank away.

"I don't think you're as smart as they say," Erik continued. "I think you're a dumb rat. I WANT YOU TO BE A RAT AND RUN AROUND THE PLAY THING LIKE IT'S A MAZE," he yelled. "I EVEN HAVE A PIECE OF CHEESE FOR YOU IF YOU DO GOOD." Erik pulled a half-melted, plastic-cheese sandwich from his jacket pocket. He picked out a quarter, a penny, a paper clip, and a gum-wrapper with old gum in it, and peeled back the squished slices of bread to show Rodan his rubbery cheesey reward.

Rodan's face turned red – as red as his hands. He had used them as brake pads to stop his fall.

Pugh ran to the play structure to see if Miles could come up with a rescue plan.

Miles was sitting in his usual spot at the bottom of the silver slide, with a book balanced on his knees. Even with a million kids around him his eyes wouldn't leave the page. And he never got hit by anyone coming down the slide. When Miles felt the vibration a kid's bum made when it hit metal, he'd stand up and move to the side. After the kid shot off the end, Miles would sit back

down. One day Pugh had counted. Miles had moved 163 times and read seven chapters in 42 minutes.

"Miles . . . MILES . . . **MILES!**" Pugh yelled.

Miles jerked his head up. A kid came zooming down the slide and leapfrogged over the distracted Miles.

Pugh grabbed Miles and pulled him behind the wall of tires.

"Did you see who yelled at me?" Miles asked and went back to reading.

"It was me!" Pugh snatched the book and held it at his side, "I've got something for you."

"Food or books?" Miles started to look interested.

"A problem."

"Math or personal?"

"Pest control." Pugh pointed through the tire. "Erik is bringing Rodan over here to make him run like a rat."

Miles sighed. He looked at the book Pugh was holding hostage. He took off his glasses and rubbed his left eyebrow. A good eyebrow massage helped him think. "First we see if we can talk Erik out of it. With the right motivation. . . ."

Pugh looked doubtful. "What's plan B?"

"We let Rodan run," Miles decided. "Just like in a real experiment. Only I don't have a hypothesis and normally I wouldn't use an animal because it's cruel. But right now we don't have much choice." He took back his book, put his glasses on, and pulled out the watch he used for timing his speed-reading. "Let's see what Lab Rat can do."

Erik was holding Rodan by the scruff of his shirt. He dangled him over the mud puddle beneath the monkey bars.

Miles walked right up to Erik and said, "If you get caught messing with Rodan, *your own classmate*, Bellows for sure won't let us in the contest."

Erik laughed and looked Miles in the eyes. "And besides the top of your head, your point would be?"

Miles sighed, "I've got a stopwatch. Where's the start and finish?"

Erik let go of Rodan.

Rodan landed with a splash. He watched the dirty water run into his high-tops while he rubbed the blood back into his arms.

"How come you're helping me and not geeky here?" Erik gestured at Rodan.

Miles shrugged. "My dad said I should be nice to you," he answered. "He's a Buddhist and believes in being kind to all lower life forms."

"Whatever," said Erik. "Just start your timer thing when I say 'Go.'" Erik turned to Rodan who was sitting on the slide emptying his shoes, "You start running when I say 'Go.' You've got to do two laps on the ground, then hit the rope ladder, go over the swinging bridge, through the tube and back, down the fire pole, up the tire wall, across the monkey bars, down the slide, and hit the puddle. Got it?"

"Yes," Rodan said. He pulled his laces super tight and double knotted them.

"Good." Erik hung his arm over Miles' shoulder. "Me and flower bud here will be waiting for you to fall on your face and give us all a good laugh."

Rodan stared straight ahead, narrowed his eyes, and got set.

Erik smiled. "GO!"

Miles hit his stopwatch.

Rodan took off.

Everybody backed up and watched Rodan as he flew past. They were showered with woodchips as Rodan burned around the first corner. His second lap was even faster.

"Go, Lab Rat," a third-grader mumbled as Rodan scrabbled up the rope web like a spider after a fresh fly.

Rodan bounced over the bridge.

"Whoa!" someone said in awe.

Erik lost his smile.

Rodan dove into the tube and did a belly-slide to the end where he stuck his tongue out at the crowd. They all laughed. He popped up onto all fours and backed his way up the tube like a steam engine in reverse.

"GO Lab Rat! GO Lab Rat!"

Erik looked around for the cheerleaders.

Rodan wrapped his legs around the fire pole and shot to the ground, no hands. Sparks flew from the metal grommets of his shoes.

Kids jostled each other to get a better look.

Rodan climbed the tire wall faster than a chimpanzee and swung through the monkey bars like an orangutan.

The crowd inched closer and swallowed Erik and Miles.

Rodan did the slide, surfer style, flew through the air like a ski jumper, and landed like a gymnast standing up in the mud puddle.

"TIME!" Everybody yelled.

Miles squeezed through and stood beside Rodan who was breathing hard but smiling. Miles checked his watch and announced, "33.795 seconds."

"I'm next!"

"No ME!"

"I WAS HERE FIRST!"

Miles looked around for Erik.

Erik had disappeared faster than a rabbit down a hole.

Miles started the next kid.

Everyone was slapping Rodan so hard on the back that he choked. He caught his breath and asked, "Where's Erik?"

"My hypothesis," Miles declared, "is that Erik has gone somewhere to think about his future since he has decided not to be a scientist."

But no one had seen Brittany Madison Heather Wales stomp off to the office.

FUNERAL MARCH

esides Erik's failed attempt to humiliate Rodan, and Rodan's new Olympic-god status on the playground, strange things had been happening all week. The garbage can had been tipped over and it looked as if someone had held a batting practice with all the papers, wrappers, and half-eaten food. Gum hung like stretched tongues from the ceiling. Miles' books had been knocked off shelves, Pugh's pencils chewed in half, Todd's iPod with thirty-seven versions of *Waltzing Matilda* went walkabout every night and was found in a different desk every morning. Nina's collection of erasers that looked like a mouse family went missing completely. Room 207 complained loudly about having to spend half the morning cleaning up. Especially since it didn't count for the contest.

Now, Miss Chimney wasn't as old as Miss New. And she never yelled at her students like Mr. Bellows did. But sometimes Miss Chimney would say, "Room 207, if you don't quiet down, I'm going to blow my stack!" She didn't say that on Friday, though, because of the funeral.

Professor Shrimpington had taken a turn for the worse and twirled his antennae one last time. He was resting at the bottom of his fishbowl when everyone came in after morning bell. Miss Chimney told Room 207 they were going to "lay him to rest" in a better place. The school garden.

"Raise your hand if you've been to a funeral," said Miss Chimney.

Pugh put down his math homework and raised his hand, "I've been to one funeral a year since grade two, and now that I'm in grade five I estimate that by the end of high school I won't go to any more funerals

because I won't have anybody left." Pugh put his hand down and looked relieved. It's not that he didn't like his family. And math was his best subject. He just didn't like funerals.

Nina raised her hand again.

"Yes, Nina?" said Miss Chimney

"I made a cross for the Professor," said Nina. She held up a grave marker made of Popsicle sticks. "I didn't know his date of birth so I just put a question mark."

"Good thinking, Nina. X marks the spot," snickered Erik. "Now when Miss Weedwhacker lets the rug rats out of their kinder-cage, they'll know x-actly where to dig him up."

"That's not an X stupid," Olive sneered. "It's a cross like a t."

"And it was very thoughtful," added Miss Chimney.

Erik lowered himself in his seat.

Adam raised his hand. "Who's going to fish the poor bloke out?"

"Rodan, would you mind?" Miss Chimney rummaged around in her desk until she found a small green fishnet.

Rodan took it from her. He dipped the net in the bowl and bumped the body against the glass. He hesitated, "Miss Chimney, in the name of science. . . ."

Miss Chimney winced. "You'll have to find another corpse, Rodan. This one was my friend," she said, and her eyes glistened.

Rodan finally caught him and handed the net over to Juliet.

Dead bodies were about the only thing that didn't make Juliet faint. She transferred the body to the blue velvet jewelry box that held her smelling salts. She felt her father would be proud that she was carrying on the family business. Someday she would take over the Faintheart Funeral Parlor. Juliet gently folded Professor's little legs under his body. She fanned out his tail and gave it a jaunty Shrimpington flip so he looked happy. Then she tucked him in with a tissue and closed the lid silently.

Miss Chimney put on her black trench coat. "Get your coats . . . it's a lovely day for a funeral."

Miss Chimney led the procession. They transported the closed casket on a little hammock that Nina had made out of florescent pink and green cord. Hooking their baby fingers into the webbing and stretching it out between them, Nina and Samantha walked on the left of the body. Miles and Rodan on the right. Erik followed right on Rodan's heels and kept giving him a flat tire. Todd carried a shovel. The rest of the class followed at a respectable distance.

They were almost at the garden when Erik broke

the silence. "This is so lame," he said loud enough for everyone to hear. "Should've thrown him down the outhouse hole."

"Getting dumped in the dunny wouldn't be much of a send-off," Adam said, sticking out his foot to trip his brother.

"Criiiiky!" Todd cried, "You'll pay for that!" He grabbed Adam and got him into a headlock. "Say hello to Mr. Smelly Shoe." Todd whipped off his shoe and held it on Adam's face like an oxygen mask.

Principal Bellows stuck his head out his office window and yelled across the schoolyard, "You there! What are you doing?"

Todd and Adam dropped shoe and shovel and kicked them toward Erik.

"And why do you look so suspicious?"

Erik quickly hid the tools of torture behind his back so Mr. Bellows wouldn't take them away.

"You boys stay right where you are," Mr. Bellows pointed at them. "I'm coming out."

Olive turned on the boys. "Nice going, you guys!"

Nina's face changed from sad to worried, "Ah, Miss Chimney? Principal Bellows is coming," she said. "Were we supposed to get a permit or something to do this?"

"Oh, I don't know." Miss Chimney shrugged her shoulders.

Principal Bellows came rolling at great speed across the schoolyard. With his black suit, nostrils flaring and mouth open ready to yell, he looked like a furious bowling ball. "What is the meaning of all this?" He stopped just short of knocking them all down.

Everyone tried to explain at once.

"The Professor was old. . . ."

"He tripped me. . . ."

"Worst smell ever. . . ."

"I hate school."

Mr. Bellows raised his hands over his head, "Quiet everyone!" He eyed the crowd. "Who said *I hate school*?"

Erik started to raise his hand but Olive snatched it and held it down. "Oh nobody said they hate school, sir," she said sweetly. Olive squeezed Erik's fingers and started swinging their hands between them. "Erik actually said *great* school." She smiled at Mr. Bellows and batted her eyes at Erik. "Ever since he's come to Room 207 he *loves* school."

Mr. Bellows crossed his arms and puffed out his chest, "Is this true Erik?"

Olive squeezed Erik's hand so hard his knuckles cracked, "Yeah." *Crack.* "I mean, yes." *Crack crack.* "Yes, Sir!"

The principal looked puzzled. "That's certainly a change in attitude."

Olive let go of Erik's hand. "It'd be worth a couple points in the contest don't you think?"

"Maybe . . . I don't know . . . what else is going on here?" Mr. Bellows asked.

Pugh muttered under his breath, "Now we're going to get it."

Miss Chimney cleared her throat. "I'm sorry. We didn't post an announcement. I thought a private affair would be more fitting," she said, and wiped a tear from her eye. "We're on our way to bury Professor Shrimpington. Perhaps you would like to join us for the service?"

"Professor Pimpleton?" Bellows looked confused. "When did he join the staff?"

"You mean *Shrimpington*, sir," said Nina trying to be helpful.

Bellows stamped his foot. "Don't tell me the board went and hired. . . ."

"He's not a teacher, he's a shrimp," Nina interrupted.

The principal gave her a stern look. "That's a disrespectful thing to say, young lady."

Nina's shoulders sank.

Miss Chimney put a hand on Nina's arm, and looked at Principal Bellows. "Professor Shrimpington," she said patiently, "was our dearly beloved class pet who *was* a shrimp. This is his funeral." She paused and

sniffed. "We would like to start soon. The sun is almost overhead and there will be an open-casket viewing before the burial."

Mr. Bellows backed up. "Uh, well, there is no digging on school property without forms 3-17B. . . ."

Juliet brought the blue box close to his nose and waved funerary fumes in his face.

Mr. Bellows turned green around the gills. "Ah . . . I should do the paperwork."

Juliet lowered the casket. "Out of respect for Miss Chimney and her great loss you really should join all of us in our sorrow and celebration," she pronounced.

All the children said, "*Pleeease.*"

Miss Chimney chimed in. "It would mean so much to them," she said, patting Erik on the head. "They've had such a hard week not being included in the contest and having their class pet pass away."

Juliet slowly opened the velvet coffin.

"Can't . . . join you . . . this time," Mr. Bellows stammered, "but, ah, for your caring and compassion toward another creature. . . ."

CREEEEAK . . .

He gulped, "I will award you Best Classroom points." He covered his mouth and ran back to the school.

Olive waved. "Don't forget extra points for Erik's new 'tude."

"Good-oh!" Todd punched his brother, "we're back in the game!" He dodged Adam's return punch. "Just thinkin' on all that lovely ice cream makes me hungry," he licked his lips.

Everyone laughed and shook their heads.

Miss Chimney smiled and led the children to the garden, but not before she winked at Juliet.

AMADEUS

It was quiet study hour in Room 207. Everyone was reading or finishing work or recovering from the funeral. Pourquoi studied the inside of his eyelids and Butterbum had crawled between the sheets of paper in the homework bin for a snooze.

Miss Chimney sat at her desk with her head bent over Rodan's English comprehension test. She held her magnifying glass right up to her eye and peered down at the paper. Deciphering Rodan's work required all her concentration and a lot of face scrunching because Rodan had the smallest writing ever. So she didn't even look up when she heard Mozart coming from the corner of the room. "Now is not the time for piano practice, Miles," Miss Chimney said and screwed up her face to concentrate.

Miles didn't hear her. He was completely lost in the story of *Beethoven Lives Upstairs*.

Miss Chimney and Miles were the only ones not staring at the piano.

"Miles! I said now . . . Oh my," Miss Chimney said, finally looking up.

Nina tapped Miles on the shoulder. Then she pinched him. And then she yanked his hair to pull his nose out of the book.

Miles lifted his head and closed his eyes in pain, "Ow! Olive, knock it off!" He swatted at the hand that still gripped his hair. When he opened his eyes he was shocked to see it was Nina. And Nina looked even more shocked than he was.

Nina pointed to the piano.

Miles' jaw dropped and Beethoven fell to the floor.

The music continued. But the piano wasn't playing all by itself.

Erik's voice shook when he asked, "Ah . . . are cats supposed to be see-through?"

"No, Erik they are not," said Miss Chimney.

Erik moved to the edge of his seat, ready to bolt, "And are cats that aren't supposed to be see-through . . . ah, should they be playing a piano?"

"Right now no one should be playing the piano," declared Miss Chimney. She put down her marking and rose from her seat, "Especially a transparent cat."

The cat looked as if it were made of smoke. It changed from light to dark, depending on the mood of the music, as it pranced across the keys. It was conducting itself with its tail. Swish, swish. Poke the air. Swish, swish. Swing down low. Near the end, the phantom cat's tail stood straight up like a rocket at takeoff and quivered. It finished with a flourish. The cat sprang to the top of the piano, and slammed the cover over the keys with its back feet. The cat had a good stretch, reclined regally, and proceeded to lick its smoky paws with a see-through tongue.

"I guess it's finished." Juliet's eyes started to roll back into her head. "And so am I."

Nina slid her backpack across the aisle to break Juliet's fall.

The cat looked up at the sound of Juliet crashing.

"What, might I inquire, does *not* make that child faint?" the cat asked. "It seems that the slightest noise or foul smell or harsh word or something too big or any kind of life form startles the poor little muffin into a fit and she falls apart." The cat sat up straight. "The children who used to be here were tougher and quieter and, if I might add, better looking. Pity they didn't look after me better. Or I might never have been locked in here and left to perish without a thought. But then again, I would not have learned to play the piano properly. My name is Amadeus. It used to be Cheddar, but I changed it." Amadeus sneered.

Miss Chimney cleared her throat, "Welcome to Room 207 . . . Amadeus."

Amadeus tilted his head. "It is I who should welcome you, since I was here first. In fact, I have been here for more than a century." He looked up at the ceiling. "It would be quite rude of you not to provide me with a lovely host's gift. Fresh fish would be acceptable. Tinned if you must. Or a warm quail egg. Perhaps cream that has just this moment risen to the top. . . ."

Miss Chimney glanced at the empty fish bowl on her desk. Then she moved to the homework bin. She slid Butterbum out of the bin and placed her in a desk drawer, careful to leave it open a crack for air. Butterbum squealed.

Miss Chimney coughed to cover the sound of Butterbum's distress.

Amadeus looked right at the teacher and said, "I have more discerning taste than what you imply by incarcerating that overstuffed hairball. Don't you think I could have done anything I wanted to all these nights after you went home?"

Miss Chimney's hand flew to her mouth.

"The shrimp you are thinking of was good company while he lasted, but he was seven years old when you rescued him from that overcrowded tank in Pete's Pet Shop."

Miss Chimney gasped.

"Dear Lady, you are just as hopeless a fishmonger as you are a pigsmith. I have tried, on several occasions, to converse with the spoiled rodentia of your desk." Amadeus sniffed. "It had nothing to say. The larger, bald version of the little one seems to suffer from the same affliction. They are both either deaf as doorknobs or dumb as dirt."

Pourquoi, who had slept through Amadeus' insults, was awakened by his own loud snoring. He opened his eyes, stood up on all fours, then sat down again and yawned.

Amadeus shot a look at Miss Chimney. "I rest my case more securely than that pork roast rests his rump."

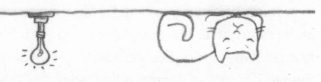

His glowing green eyes bored into Pourquoi's soft brown ones as if to melt them.

Nina stood up. "You leave him alone, you stupid old cat." She walked over to where Pourquoi sat. "Maybe Butterbum and Pourquoi are just too smart to talk to you." Nina leaned down and scratched Pourquoi behind the ears hoping to massage his brain into action.

Pourquoi looked back at the strange cat, decided it was not edible, and trotted off toward the garbage can to find a snack.

Amadeus stood up, put his tail high in the air, and wrinkled his nose as if he had smelled something horri-

ble. "Your ridiculous statement does not even warrant comment." He jumped to the floor, walked up the wall, and stretched out for a nap on the ceiling.

Far away the school bell sounded.

At lunch, everyone agreed not to talk about Amadeus –

to anyone – because if they did, Miss Chimney would probably get fired. The rest of Anna Swan would think Room 207 was crazy. You can't win a Best Classroom Contest if your classroom is full of nuts.

HARVEST FESTIVAL

After a stern talking to from Miss Chimney about the uncivilized behavior of stealing, Amadeus spent the weekend rounding up all the items he had borrowed from Room 207. He lined them up nicely on her desk, but could not do anything about the flaky dried cat spit that covered them.

On Monday morning Miss Chimney clanged the rusty cowbell that hung outside the door. The sound echoed across the staff's parking lot to the field where everyone hung out until it was time to go in to school.

Most of Anna Swan Heights headed for the big brick building while the students of Room 207 walked to their class, waving good-bye to friends and throwing insults at enemies.

Surrounded by her gang of brats, Brittany Madison Heather Wales teased Erik as he walked by. "What's it like going from the *bullpen* to a *PIGSTY?*" The girls snorted and pranced, laughing and snickering.

Erik turned red and tuned in Pugh on his radar.

Olive yelled to Mark Woolly, "Your head looks stupid in that hat!" Olive stuck her tongue out at Mark and pointed to the top of his head. She wanted to pick a fight with him so she could spend the day in the principal's office instead of Room 207 with the freaky cat.

Nina collected the autumn leaves to give to Miss Chimney.

Todd kicked a soccer ball to Adam.

Erik caught up with Pugh and kicked him all the way to the schoolhouse.

The students of Room 207 filed into the old building.

"I have a very exciting project to announce." Miss Chimney closed the door behind them.

"Oh-oh," Miles said as he found his seat. He liked Miss Chimney, but whenever a teacher said they had an "exciting project" it meant that the next two weeks of your life were going to be more boring than a lecture from your sister on how to dry nail polish.

Miss Chimney walked to the front of the room and held her hand up as the signal for quiet. "Even though we are physically separated from Anna Swan

Heights Public School we are still part of it *and* the contest, so that means we will be participating in this year's Fall Fling."

Groans filled the room.

"It counts for one-third of our Best Classroom points," Miss Chimney reminded them.

Room 207 groaned again – this time the type of groans you hear in hospitals.

Miss Chimney decided her students must be bloated from their breakfasts. She retrieved the first aid shoebox and found the Good Thief Stomach Remedy: Guaranteed to clean you out in no time. She shook the bottle and the class cringed. "Oh, I think you'll like the theme this year. It's Harvest Festival and. . .'"

"How original," Olive interrupted. "Last year it was the Festival of Harvests."

Rodan chimed in. "Celebration of the Harvest's Bounty was the year before that."

"When I was in kindergarten I think it was called Good Gourd, It's Fall Again because that's all I remember Miss MacDonald ever saying," Pugh added.

Miss Chimney folded her hands in front of her and looked proudly at her class. "What good memories you all have. But you won't need them for this year's production because no one will have any lines."

"No singing?" Nina was disappointed.

"No singing. That would be unrealistic," said Miss Chimney.

Juliet was suspicious. She was afraid to get her hopes up too high. The hope she got up just a little was that maybe they wouldn't have to go on stage at all. She suffered from severe stage fright. "Why no singing?" Juliet asked.

"Because vegetables don't sing, but you will look boun- tiful when you dance." Miss Chimney did a perfect pirouette.

Juliet's eyes fluttered and her head hit the desk.

Pourquoi trotted over, belly swinging from side to side, to see if Juliet had dropped anything good to eat.

Erik grinned and stuck his foot out to trip up the pig. But Pourquoi thought that Erik was offering him a seat. So he settled the toothless end of himself on Erik's new high-tops.

"You disgusting pig!" Erik stopped smiling. He poked at Pourquoi's soft underbelly with his toe. "How about a nice plump pork chop to go with all those vegetables?"

Pourquoi squealed, jumped up, did his usual exit

stage left through his mud flap, and hid in the manure pile.

Nina narrowed her eyes at Erik. "Why don't you pick on someone your own shoe size?"

Erik laughed. "I would, except I'm stuck here in the middle of a shrimp fest." The minute Erik said it he regretted it and became as quiet as the rest of the class. He knew what they were all thinking. He was the biggest kid in the class. He was the biggest fifth grader in the whole school, because he was supposed to be in sixth grade. He'd been held back because he couldn't read. If anybody knew, nobody said so. They didn't tease him about not being able to hit the books because he could pound kids into the ground with no problem.

Miss Chimney thought her students were worried about the project, "You have a choice. You can be unusual veggies or traditional vegetables," she said brightly, trying to lift their spirits.

Erik was glad for the change of subject. "I *traditionally hate* brussels sprouts," he said under his breath.

Miss Chimney only heard "I" and "brussels sprouts." "Good for you, Erik. Brussels sprouts are an under-appreciated, yet noble vegetable. Lots of calcium and *ohhh* the perfumed scent they release upon boiling." She closed her eyes and inhaled deeply.

Adam rubbed circles on his stomach and whispered to Todd, "When you cover them in chocolate – yummy!"

Pugh gagged thinking about his dad's favorite vegetable. "They're good for hiding under mashed potatoes," he offered.

Olive raised her hand.

"Yes, Olive?" Miss Chimney asked.

"What did you mean by unusual vegetables?"

"Well, you have the ordinary ones like corn, peas, and carrots. . . ."

Butterbum whistled at her highest octave. "Carrots" was the only word she knew. She poked her head out of the first aid shoebox she had been rummaging around in to look for her treat.

"Yes, Butterbum, you can be a carrot." Miss Chimney patted the little pig on the head, "but some of you might prefer to be something exotic like the beret-capped

okra, the aromatic garlic shoot, or the young and robust rapini." Miss Chimney was happy that her students' interest in vegetables was picking up steam.

"Frijoles!" José yelled and jumped out of his seat.

"That better not be a swear word, José." Miss Chimney frowned.

"No, no Senora Chiminea. Frijoles are refried beans."

"Well, beans are *leguuummes*," she told him. "Perhaps you could think of something else."

Rodan who always liked more complicated projects asked, "What about cauliflower with cheese sauce?"

Miss Chimney pursed her lips and rubbed her chin in thought. "That could be very interesting, Rodan. Especially since all of your costumes are to be made from recycled materials you can find at home."

Jaws dropped and faces fell lower than Erik's grades.

"This project will constitute 20 percent of your first report card. And that's not the best part."

"Here it comes . . ." whispered Miles, ". . . the nail in the coffin."

"You can reuse your creations for Halloween," Miss Chimney finished triumphantly.

Amadeus chuckled. "Hilarious!" He said behind his paw.

Miles was speechless. He had been wrong. He felt bad. Real bad. This was not going to be more boring than watching nail polish dry. This project was about embarrassment. Definitely going-for-a-record, never-to-be-beaten, *the* most embarrassing project ever assigned to any grade five class anywhere. And he would never live it down but it didn't matter. Because he was going to die on stage as a bountiful broccoli in front of all his friends.

OLIVE'S HOMEWORK

Olive and Erik refused to do the vegetable costumes, so Miss Chimney had assigned them essays instead. Bonus points were going to be awarded to the class that wrote the best essay. The topic was harvesting man-made materials to help the environment. Erik changed his mind and decided he would rather be a brussels sprout than a bookworm.

Olive was researching the recycling of diapers for her paper.

"This homework stinks," muttered Olive at her bedroom wall.

The essay was due the next day.

"My brain is constipated!" Olive sharpened her pencil for the eleventh time. She was almost down to the metal part that held the red eraser. She could have

ground her homework to a halt by jamming the last bit
of her pencil into the electric sharpener, but then her
mom would have run into the room and grounded Olive.
Olive still wouldn't have been able to play her favorite
video game, Surfing Samurai Mini-Monkey Reef Savers,
on the new super-huge, super-flat-screen TV her father
got for his birthday. The thought of it made her mad. Not
her father's birthday, of course. It was the not being able
to play her game because of the assignment. It made her
want to recycle her pencil into sawdust.

"Stupid. Stupid. *Stupid* paper!" screamed Olive.

No one in Olive's family was allowed to use the "S"
word. Every time someone did, they had to put a quarter
into a special jar. Olive got up, went to her pickle bank
and withdrew four quarters. She walked downstairs to
the kitchen and deposited three of them.

"Stupid jar!" Olive dropped in the last quarter.

She cut herself a piece of white cake and made a glass of chocolate milk. Everyone in Olive's family was allowed to have desert or junk food anytime they wanted to. They just weren't allowed to say the "S" word.

Olive sat at the kitchen table and read the seven newspaper articles that she knew her mom had purposely cut out and *accidentally* left for her to read. There was all sorts of stuff in the local paper about diaper recycling. The town council was considering allowing a company that recycles used diapers (the company's name was CRUD) to come and build their plant on the edge of city limits. The plant would help provide jobs for the people who were put out of work when the baby food factory closed down. CRUD could have used the baby food factory building, but it was being converted into a doggie daycare.

SHOWTIME

T he audience was buzzing.

Miss Weedwhacker's junior-kindergarten class had been the first act on stage. They performed their original piece, *Be Kind To Broccoli From the Farm*, to a prerecorded version of *Old MacDonald*. Two little kids fell off the stage. And one big kid wet his pants.

Behind the stage curtain, Olive hiked up the overalls Miss Chimney had made her wear. "NOT fair. I did the essay and you said I didn't have to wear a costume or say any lines," she whined.

Miss Chimney adjusted Olive's straw hat. "It's not a costume. It's what farmers wear, and someone has to introduce our vegetables and our Basket of Bounty."

Olive cursed under her breath. "Otherwise no one would know what the hell they are."

"Heck, Olive, heck!" corrected Miss Chimney as she pushed Olive on stage to the microphone. "Farmers say 'Heck.'"

Adam pranced by all dressed in purple and blew a kiss at Olive. "I'm a passion fruit." He winked at her.

"Go to heck!"

A grade three stagehand, Arnie Snots, dragged Pourquoi on a leash toward Olive. The grade four props master, Missy MacQuire, brought Olive her pitchfork.

The curtains parted and – except for Pourquoi – Olive was alone onstage. She held Pourquoi's leash and the pitchfork in one hand and picked up the script from the podium with the other. She cleared her throat. "Lentils and Wheat Germ," Olive said into the microphone. Olive looked to the wings. "Who wrote this crapola?" she hissed.

"Olive!" Miss Chimney warned from backstage.

"I mean *granola*."

The audience laughed.

"Welcome to Room 207's Basket of Bounty presentation." Olive rolled her eyes. "I'm Olive Farmer. . . ."

"You're an olive farmer?" Mark Woolly heckled from the front row.

"No!" Olive checked the script and glared back-stage, "I'm . . . Fanny Farmer?"

"You farm fannies?" Mark asked, and the audience laughed again.

Olive stared Mark down. "Yeah, and yours is lookin' pretty ripe." She stabbed her pitchfork into the hard-wood floor.

The audience stopped laughing. Mark sat back and squirmed in his seat.

Olive threw away the script. "Now that I have your attention, and since I don't have a choice, let me introduce the stup ..." Olive caught her mother's eye, "... the stu-*PENDOUS* vegetables."

The stagehands wheeled out a piece of plywood cut and painted to look like a huge basket.

Olive shook her head. "Our first guess, ah, guest is Miles. ..."

Miles came on stage with pillows strapped to his body with bungee cords.

Olive stared at Miles. "... Miles, the mashed potato?"

He gave her the thumbs-up and jumped behind the plywood to look like he had landed in the basket.

"Rodan is. ..."

Rodan shuffled out wrapped from head to toe in tinfoil.

"Baked potato," he whispered to Olive.

Olive covered the microphone. "You look like a beacon for the Mothership."

Olive turned to the audience. "Rodan is a baked potato ... I guess potatoes are big this year."

Rodan fell into the basket and the audience howled.

Olive was starting to enjoy herself. "Okay, next we have Nina. ..."

Nina waltzed out wearing green ballet shoes, green tights, a green leotard, and a shiny green zip-up jacket.

She unzipped her coat and there was Butterbum stuffed into a ball of green wool.

"Nina and Butterbum," Olive announced. "One pea and a pod. Aren't they cute? How about a big hand for Nina and her green pea!"

The kindergartners cracked up. The parents made faces.

Olive looked stage left. José was ready and he couldn't have looked happier.

Olive didn't have a clue what he was supposed to be. "This next one needs no introduction," she told the crowd.

José did a beautiful dance to center stage trailing a puffy, dark green sweater and a wrinkled brown trench coat, "I am the chili rellano," he announced. "First I am the cheese," he ran his hands down front of the pale yellow sweatshirt he wore, "that is stuffed inside the pepper." He pulled the sweater over his head. "And then I am rolled in the flour and boiled in the oil!" He put on the trench coat and took a deep bow.

The crowd went wild. José's mom and dad whistled.

Juliet waddled out in an orange garbage bag stuffed with newspapers and a black jack-o-lantern face painted on the front. Her parents stood at the edge of the stage ready to catch her.

"Fall's finest . . ." Olive declared, ". . . the pumpkin!"

Everyone cheered.

Todd walked on stage in blue jeans and a striped T-shirt and the top of a pineapple duct-taped to his head.

The crowd fell silent.

"ASPARAGUS!" Todd yelled at them.

Samantha stumbled on to the stage. She wore white slippers and light green flannel pajamas. Above her head she drowsily waved dark green gloves.

Samantha yawned.

Olive took her cue, "After sleeping all winter . . . the spring onion!"

Erik appeared from the other side of the stage. He had purple balloons stamped with 'Happy Birthday' taped to his clothes. His shoes were covered in triple-chocolate cake and rocky road ice cream.

Olive remembered what he said he was going to be. "Brussels sprouts!"

Pugh joined the rest of his class wearing a long red nightshirt and a green hat. "Plum tomato," he told Olive.

Mark heard him. "Looks like a *dumb* tomato!"

Olive saw red. "I warned you Woolly!" She lunged for him. Pourquoi smelled the cake stuck to the bottom of Erik's shoes and charged. He jerked Olive back toward the basket. Olive stabbed Todd in the asparagus and Todd's pineapple top punctured Erik's balloons.

All heck broke loose.

The audience howled, dogs barked from three blocks away, and the show ended early.

Room 207 received the highest rating on the applause-o-meter and got Best in Show.

In the parking lot the parents agreed that it was the most educational and entertaining pageant yet.

GAZUND-TIGHT!

"Late again, Samantha?" Miss Chimney raised her eyebrows.

"Our refrigerator broke and Mom yelled 'Save the sour cream!' so Dad put the air conditioner in my room because it's the smallest." Samantha sighed. "All the food from the fridge went under my bed. I was up all night freezing. I'm sorry I'm late."

"I'm sorry that you didn't bring your air conditioner with you." Miss Chimney mopped her brow.

Tatamagouche was having a record-breaking heat spell. The weatherman had said it was hotter than an oven in "H E double hockey sticks."

Pourquoi was the only one not bothered. He lounged in front of Miss Chimney's desk sucking and slurping and munching on a mango pit. Butterbum watched from above. She stretched herself out like a Slinky, trying to keep her bum in the middle of the desk as she gripped the edge with her front paws and peered down at Pourquoi. These were their assigned spots. Butterbum now spent most of her days on top of the teacher's desk because Miles found out that guinea pigs were originally from the Andes. Also, Pourquoi had run her over thirteen times since the beginning of school. And since the beginning of school, Pourquoi didn't care where he sat, even if it was on Butterbum.

"Since the temperature is at the boiling point," said Miss Chimney, looking at her new giant thermometer that bubbled like a lava lamp, "and most of you are more wilted than yesterday's lettuce, I think we should read some cold books."

Nina's hand shot up. "I know one. It's called *What Happens When the Light Goes Off – The Inside Story of the Fridge.*"

"Oh, yes, Nina, I've read that one. I love mysteries that make you all shivery, but I was thinking more along the lines of history. I've got some excellent books on the Ice Age. And I have them all prepared for you." Miss Chimney lugged a large blue cooler that was covered in white icicles from the cloakroom. She used a hammer and chisel to remove the lid. Icy mist squirted from the sides. "Dig in!" She flopped into her chair and fanned herself.

Miles was the first one to grab a frosty book. When he tried to open it his fingers stuck to the cover. He blew hot breath on his hands and only succeeded in thawing the title, *The Iceman Cometh*. Miles went back to his seat to wait.

Erik tripped Miles as he went by. "Watch your step, *stupid*," he muttered. Erik covered his hands with his sleeves and grabbed a big book he planned to throw at Pugh. Erik licked his book to see if his tongue would freeze to it. Then he had to visit Nurse Payne in her office so she could use her blow-dryer and a paint scraper borrowed from Mr. Drum, the janitor, to free Erik's tongue from *Trapped In Ice*. Everyone said that was the closest Erik was ever going to get to having his nose stuck in a book.

After that Nina grabbed the ancient black tongs from the wall beside the woodstove and started delivering books to everyone's desk.

Sleeping On Ice was the name of Samantha's book. "Aaahhh," Samantha sighed. She put the sweater she'd worn this morning over the book. Nearly freezing to death all night had made her tired so she put her head down on her chilly pillow and snored.

Amadeus found the music to *Cat on a Hot Tin Roof* and played with heated passion, just to taunt the children.

Everyone else waved their hands over their books and tried to create cool breezes.

Miles finally got his hands unglued. A puddle had formed on his desk and cold water was dripping on his knee.

"*Aachoo!*"

Miles jumped.

"Bless you, Miles!" said Miss Chimney.

"I didn't. . . ." Miles didn't finish his sentence.

Because it wasn't Miles who had sneezed.

It was his desk.

PAYNE AND PANIC

Next day Miles still hadn't said anything about his sneezing desk. He was freaked out. All he wanted to do was get lost in a book and forget that yesterday ever happened.

But today was Tuesday. And Tuesday was desk clean-out day.

"Room 207, I would like to remind you that Pourquoi is happy to recycle any unwanted contents," Miss Chimney said. "Please open your desktops for inspection."

The more Miles thought about what might be in his desk, the more he didn't want it inspected. Yesterday cold water dripped on his knee and his desk had sneezed. Today cold sweat dripped off his brow and he felt sick.

Miss Chimney walked toward him. "Is there a reason you aren't participating today Miles?" She cocked her head to the side and gave him a crooked smile.

"No ma'am," Miles leaned forward across his desk and gripped the edges. He sighed as he laid his cheek on the wooden top and closed his eyes.

"Ma'am?" repeated Miss Chimney. "Something must *really* be wrong." She reached her hand out and lifted Miles' chin. Then she placed her other hand on his forehead. "Oh my. You're hotter than Helios!"

Nina's hand shot up like a rocket. "I'll take him to see Nurse Payne."

"That's a good idea." Erik stuck his swollen, purple tongue out at Miles.

"It *is* a good idea Erik. Better than the one you had yesterday," said Miss Chimney.

Miles was terrified of going to Nurse Payne's infirmary. There were rumors on the playground about how Nurse Payne took temperatures. He didn't want to learn the truth, but if he stayed in class he'd have to learn about something worse – what makes a desk sneeze.

Nina took Miles by the arm and led him out of Room 207 across the soccer field, through the playground, into the school, and down the stairs into the basement. Nina sang *Somewhere Over The Rainbow* the whole way.

Miles kept singing *If I Only Had A Brain* in his head and wishing he did because then maybe he could figure some way out of this trip to the dungeon.

Too late. They had arrived.

Nina knocked on the stainless, absolutely stainless, no-fingerprints-anywhere door. It flew open and something reached out, grabbed Nina, and dragged her inside.

Miles wanted to run. He wanted to run more than he wanted a puppy for Christmas and books for his birthday. But the screaming from inside the room paralyzed him.

"NOT ME! NOT ME! MILES! OUTSIDE!"

The door opened with a whoosh of antiseptic air. Nina was tossed out and Miles disappeared behind the door faster than a fly down a Venus'-flytrap.

"What is wrong with you?" Nurse Payne demanded.

Miles just stood there with his eyes bugging out.

"Something wrong with your ice-cream licker?"

Miles remembered Erik's swollen tongue. Miles stuck his tongue out quickly so Nurse Payne wouldn't get any ideas – or tools from Mr. Drum.

"Well? Out with it. Tell me your problem before I give you one myself."

"I . . . I . . . I," Miles stammered.

"Your eyes? Yes they do look extra large." Nurse Payne turned and opened a glass cabinet with glass jars of blue liquid with things floating in them. "These should be the right size."

Miles backed against the wall and managed to get out a whole sentence, "Miss Chimney said I had a fever."

"Oh. Then we won't need these," said Nurse Payne.

Miles heard a little clink, but since the nurse still had her back to him, he couldn't see what she had dropped in the jar.

"Mr. Drum borrowed my digital thermometer to check the furnace. I'll have to take your temperature the old-fashioned way." Nurse Payne unscrewed the lid off another jar.

Miles stood with his hands behind him, covering his backside, as if he had to go to the boy's room really badly.

Nurse Payne spun around to face him and held up a short glass stick with a red bulb at the end. "Get ready!" She fired it like a dart at Miles.

Miles opened his mouth just in time. He was so relieved he slumped to the floor as if he'd been harpooned.

The phone on Nurse Payne's desk rang. She swooped down on it and snatched up the receiver like an eagle catches fish. "Payne speaking. Hello? HELLO!"

"Nurse Payne? Miss Chimney here. Can you hear me now? I'm on Erik's cell phone. Oh, apparently it's not Erik's but he says I can use it anyway."

"Why are you calling? I'm busy!" Nurse Payne screeched.

Miss Chimney thought there must be a bad connection so she yelled back, "I'm calling about Miles. How is his fever?"

Nurse Payne flew at Miles and swiped the thermometer from between his lips with her free hand. "Miss Chimney, your diagnosis was wrong. Miles does not have a fever. He has weak knees and a blockage that is stopping any blood from reaching his face. I'll give him my own tonic. *That* should fix him."

"What should I do if it doesn't?" Miss Chimney asked.

"My tonic has never failed," Nurse Payne declared. "It fixes all the sick students. I never see them twice."

"Please tell Miles we look forward to seeing him and that his classmates have a surprise waiting."

Miles heard Miss Chimney say this directly because Nurse Payne had handed him the phone while she unscrewed the cap off an old milk jug that was filled with reddish-brown liquid the color of dried blood. She shook up the tonic, plugged Mile's nose, which made him open his mouth, and poured half the jug down his throat.

It tasted worse than if someone put fish heads and pond scum and your brother's underwear into a blender, hit puree, and made you drink it.

"I'll be right there Miss Chimney," Miles choked into the phone.

Nurse Payne picked Miles up by the arm, threw him out into the hall, and slammed the door behind him.

"Are you okay, Miles?" Nina whispered.

"I've never felt worse in my life."

"Maybe this will make you feel better. I ran back to the class while I was waiting and guess what? Todd and Adam cleaned your desk for you and . . . you won't believe what they found!"

DISAPPEARING
ACT

"What is it?" Todd asked.

"I wish I knew," Miles said.

"Where did it come from?" Adam whispered.

"Behind my ear." Miles stared into the desk.

"You should go see a doctor," Todd and Adam blurted out at the same time.

What they wanted a doctor to see was lying in the corner of Miles' desk. It was paler than when Miles had picked it up from the wreck of the original Room 207. There it had looked like melted lime Jell-O. Now it looked more like slow-boiling banana custard. And it was bubbling some kind of clear-green snotty stuff.

The slime coughed and blew all the papers Todd and

Adam had organized for Miles into another mess inside his desk.

Miss Chimney looked up from her desk. "Miles, are you sure you're feeling okay?"

"Uhh . . . I'm fine."

"You don't look fine." Miss Chimney was worried. "Maybe you should go back to Nurse Payne."

"NO! . . . I mean . . . no thank you." Miles panicked. "One dose of her tonic was enough."

Miss Chimney nodded in agreement. "She said that's all it would take." She went back to making more Mad Math Minute sheets for next Monday.

The slime gave another weaker cough and Miles, Todd, and Adam slammed the desktop down.

Butterbum squealed at the loud noise and jumped into Miss Chimney's junk drawer.

Pourquoi lumbered up from in front of the teacher's desk and gave a surprised snort.

"Holy cow, look at the size of that pig!" Miles exclaimed.

Todd put his arms out and puffed up his chest and cheeks. "Pourquoi looks like the balloon they fly over the Piggly Wiggly supermarket when it's having a big sale."

"And he's gonna burst if he doesn't take a break," said Adam. "He's been eating everyone's leftovers. You know, leftover food, homework, tests, and newsletters that were supposed to go home. He wolfed down Pugh's math sheets, Samantha's late slips gave him indigestion, Rodan's science homework gave him a case of bad gas, and Erik's spelling tests almost killed him." Adam rolled his head to the side, showed the whites of his eyes, and stuck out his tongue.

Todd laughed. "He loves your stuff, but with that slime on it we were afraid to give him any. We didn't know what it would do to the poor guy."

The three boys watched as Pourquoi waddled to the hole in the wall that lead to his own private bathroom – the manure pile.

Snuffling sounds from inside the desk reminded them of their problem.

"We've got to do something with this thing. When I took it the first day of school I thought maybe Rodan could analyze it. When Nurse Payne came to check us for dust," Miles said with a shiver, "I hid it in my desk and forgot about it. Now it's bigger and it has a cold."

Todd tapped his fingers on the desktop to drown out the sickly noises the slime was making, "Let's just toss everything in your desk in the rubbish bin. Pourquoi doesn't go in it anymore since Miss Chimney sprayed him with the fire extinguisher. We'll hide the bin with goop in the closet and bring in the one from beside the outhouse. Nobody uses it anyway. We'll swap them back again tomorrow after soccer practice. Mr. Drum will take the rubbish out that night and the big hairy guys with the truck will empty the dumpsters on Friday." Todd brushed his hands off. "Problem solved."

"Sounds good to me." Miles smiled.

Adam nodded and went to get the garbage can. He grabbed the fly swatter in case they needed to use it as a spatula.

Adam and Todd lifted the desk while Miles held the top open. Bookmarks, book reviews, and lists of the books he'd read and all the ones he was going to read, plus every book report he'd done since the beginning of school poured into the can.

Miles winced.

The slime slid into a sad slurpy heap on top of the pile of papers.

"Bring that can right over here, boys. I'm going to clean out my desk too." Miss Chimney gave a little laugh. "If I'm to live by the sword then I guess I have to die by it."

The three boys froze in mid-footstep.

Todd panicked. He hadn't thought of Miss Chimney becoming a clean freak. She had never cleaned her desk before. Beside him Juliet was turned around in her seat and talking to Nina. Juliet's journal was lying on her

desk. "Sorry Jules," he whispered as he grabbed it and threw it on top of the slime.

Adam winked at Todd.

Miles helped them carry the can to Miss Chimney's desk. They were halfway across the room when Pourquoi's door mud flap slapped. He trotted toward them looking thinner and feeling like a new pig. He sniffed the air and his eyes opened wide. Pourquoi smelled Juliet's journal. Her writing was divine, delicious, irresistible. He looked at Miss Chimney.

"Pourquoi, don't you even think about it. You've had enough fiber for one day." Miss Chimney glared at him.

Pourquoi glared back with try-to-stop-me eyes and before Miss Chimney could get her hands on the extinguisher he made a beeline for the boys. They dropped their load and Miss Chimney jumped up and over her desk to get between the pig and the trash – she was an animal lover and hated to see a good pig go to waste. Pourquoi didn't care, he picked up speed and was a blur by the time he hit the afterburners and flew straight into Miss Chimney's arms. His momentum carried them both into the can.

Then they were gone.

HERE HE COMES

E verything seemed to happen in slow motion.

The slime grew to ten times its former size.

Then it let out the longest, stinkiest burp in the history of Anna Swan Heights.

A cloud of green gas floated to the ceiling, leaving behind the deflated slime. Butterbum passed out.

Olive said a swear word.

Todd started sucking his thumb.

Adam smacked Todd's hand away from his mouth.

A trickling of water came from the back of the room. Rodan hadn't quite wet his pants but he had spilled an experiment.

Juliet didn't faint, but she got the hiccups.

The girls started crying.

The boys felt like crying.

Except Erik. Erik was laughing. The kind of laugh that was mean and made you wish that something bad would happen to the person who was laughing.

Miles rubbed his bald spot where the hair had never grown back. He was the least shocked and the first to recover because he had a heads-up as to the slime's ability to eat human stuff. "This is not good."

Juliet kept staring at the last place she had seen her teacher and the second-fastest potbellied pig. "This . . . *hiccup* . . . is . . . *hiccup* . . . the worst . . . *hiccup* . . . not-good I've ever seen." Which was saying something, considering the business Juliet's family was in.

Nina got up and stuck her face close to the slime and yelled, "Miss Chimney? MISS CHIMNEY? Can you hear me?"

Nothing happened.

Nina tried again. "Say something or jiggle if you can hear me."

The slime remained silent and smooth. But it was changing color. It had gone from a phlegmy yellow to bright lime green. Waves of pink rippled along its surface.

Erik stood behind Nina and sneered over her shoulder. "Looks like it enjoyed its lunch of stupid teacher and side of stupid pig."

Nina turned around and pushed Erik hard enough to knock him down. She stood over him. "Maybe I should feed it *you* for dessert."

Erik's face turned red. "You and whose army?"

Olive marched over and put a regulation army boot on Erik's chest as he tried to get up. The rest of the class left their seats and surrounded him.

"I was just saying now that she's gone, we can do what we want," Erik explained in the friendliest voice he had ever used.

"We want to get her back!" Nina said. The others nodded.

Rodan had left the mess at his desk and was busy poking the slime with a ruler. "At the moment, it would be more logical if we could figure out where she went. We will assume that Pourquoi has gone to the same place."

"Hola! chicos and chicas!" José was at the window. "I don't know where Senorita Chimney and her little piggie they are gone, but I see who is coming faster than a matador being chased by a bull . . . Señor Blueberry." José pointed out the window at Mr. Bellows charging across the soccer field toward them.

BLUEBERRY BELLOWS AND PURPLE BOOTS

Todd, Adam, and Miles grunted as they moved the trash can toward the closet. Trying not to jiggle or wobble or upset the slime was hard work.

Adam yelped when they stopped for a second and the can was dropped on his big toe. "This thing is three times heavier than it was before."

Rodan was following alongside like they were transporting a patient for an emergency operation. "The increased weight of the slime is a positive sign."

"It's not positive for the ones who have to lug it around," Todd huffed.

Rodan smiled. "But it is for Miss Chimney and Pourquoi. If the slime has ingested them as food for energy consumption purposes . . ." he sighed like this was so obvious, ". . . then it hasn't started the process of breaking down flesh and digesting it."

Samantha had inched forward to see the slime. She heard Rodan's words of encouragement, thought of the worms in a cemetery, and sagged to the floor.

Juliet looked down at her. "Bad time for a snooze, Sam."

"Get her up!" Olive screamed. "We have to look normal!"

Juliet poked Samantha with a pencil. "Dead to the world."

Nina ran to her cubby and grabbed the props she was going to use for a talk on safety. She put a bicycle helmet on Samantha and dragged her, head bumping along the floor, to her desk. Nina got her into a life jacket and propped her up against the back of her seat.

Olive took her foot off of Erik and let him get up, but not before threatening him. "One word out of your mouth to Bellows and you're gonna be tasting a boot leather and toenail sandwich."

Pugh took an airsick bag from his desk. "Bellows is going to want to talk to Miss Chimney." He bent over with his head between his knees, assuming the crash position.

Olive let Erik up and started barking orders. "Erik you're the biggest so you're going to have to be Miss C."

Olive ran to the old wardrobe and grabbed Miss Chimney's big pink raincoat and purple rubber boots with yellow duckies all over them.

Erik dusted off his T-shirt and laughed. "What're *you* going to do to me if I don't?"

Olive got in his face, nose-to-nose. She pushed the coat and boots into his hands, "*Who* do you think we'll blame? And what do you think *they'll* do to *you* when they find out Miss C. is missing?"

The smile left Erik's face faster than he could get the boots on.

Olive took up the roll of drill sergeant. "You two!" she barked at Nina and Juliet, "shut the door and keep it shut till we're out the window. And stall Bellows until we're in position."

Nina and Juliet didn't know what position that was, but they were too afraid to ask.

"He's almost here!" José's voice rose.

Todd and Miles pushed Erik out the window closest to Pourquoi's bathroom. Erik landed on his head, just missing a pile of pig poo.

Adam gave Olive a leg up to follow Erik and she scrambled out the window with a grunt.

Nina and Juliet latched the door and put all their weight against it in case the rusty bolt didn't hold. Overhead they heard a hissing laugh.

Amadeus grinned down at them from the rafters.

The girls gave him the evil-eye treatment and braced themselves.

Mr. Bellows hit the door at full speed, expecting it to fly open. He bounced off instead. While the principal rolled around trying to sort himself out, Nina slid the bolt back. On his second attempt to enter Room 207, Mr. Bellows burst through the door, flattening Nina behind it.

Juliet jumped out of the way. "Good afternoon, Blu ... Mr. Bellows. Sorry about the door. We were going to open it for you. The latch is a bit sticky," she said, as sweet as honey.

Nina moaned and the door creaked as she pushed it away. The hit she'd taken had straightened her bangs and ironed out the wrinkles in her T-shirt.

Mr. Bellows didn't recognize the new Nina. "Who are you, young lady?"

"I'm Nina. Remember me? We met when you first brought Erik to Room 207."

Mr. Bellows frowned. "Yes, I remember you now. Trying to oil the hinges you tripped me up instead. You obviously have a thing about hanging around doors. Very unsafe."

"Yes, sir," said Nina. "We're having a presentation today by Samantha, our safety monitor." She pointed to Samantha who was still passed out. "Ah . . . she's just getting ready by meditating on the merits of safety," Nina stalled. "You probably want to join us since you're the principal and responsible for our safety and judging the contest. . . ."

Amadeus was lying on the old timber above the principal's head like a jaguar lounges in a tree. He started to tap Mr. Bellows on the head with the tip of his tail.

"What . . ." Mr. Bellows waved his hands over his head, ". . . juggling contest?"

"*Judging* the contest." Nina winced.

The cat tapped faster and in different spots. Mr. Bellows waved more feverishly. "Later," he said dismissively, and spared one hand to shoo her. "Go sit. And stay as far away from me as possible. You too, Jackie."

"It's Juliet, sir."

"Whatever." He glared at the students standing around looking like they weren't doing anything. "Find your seats. And where is Miss Chimney?" Bellows looked up as if expecting to see that she was the one sticking something fuzzy in his ear.

Amadeus evaporated.

The students scrambled into the closest seats and held their breath.

"Well?"

They just stared at him. He was scary standing there all dusty in his black suit and vest, with his dark hair slicked back and a new goatee on his chin that he thought made him look cool. Instead, he reminded everyone very much of a fat Dracula who had just climbed out of an old coffin.

"IS SHE HERE!??" He yelled as if the class were half deaf.

Butterbum roused herself from her daze. She let go a carrot-curdling squeal and bared her teeth at the monster.

Mr. Bellows didn't know about Butterbum. He swiped the fly swatter off a desk and raised it high above his shoulder. "Everyone stay still . . . dangerous vermin."

"Don't!" Nina sprinted toward Butterbum and snatched her off the teacher's desk. As she raced past

Mr. Bellows, she bumped his arm and he smacked himself a good one on the back of his head.

"For heaven sakes, Nancy! What is your problem?"

"Nina, sir." Butterbum's short little legs pedaled madly in mid-air and her squeal became more indignant at being held up for display. "This is Butterbum. She's a guinea pig."

"This is *exactly* what I need to talk to Miss Chimney about. I've had some strange phone calls from parents saying that Room 207 is a pigsty. They want it torn down."

Brittany Madison Heather Wales appeared out of nowhere in the doorway waving a white piece of paper, "I have a petition for demolition signed by all the *theys*."

Erik and Olive heard this through the window. "Yes!" Erik said, under his breath and pumped his fist.

Olive bristled and threw a shovel at him.

"Ouch!"

"Sorry," she whispered, but she really wasn't. "Keep your back to the window and act like Miss C. turning over the manure pile."

"No way!"

Olive didn't answer. She threw a flowerpot at him.

Erik turned around to miss it.

Just in time, because the noise drew the principal,

Brittany Madison Heather Wales, and everyone else to the window.

They had stalled Mr. Bellows as long as they could. From behind, Erik looked like Miss Chimney, planted in the manure pile and digging a hole to China. Nina hoped this was what Olive meant by being in position. Nina yelled out the window, "Miss Chimney? Principal Bellows wants to talk to you."

Miss Chimney waved a 'come here' signal without turning around.

"You want him to come out to the manure pile to you?" Nina interpreted, thinking this was a brilliant idea since Mr. Bellows probably wouldn't set a foot out there even if his own mother was being buried alive.

As if they had staged a play, Erik nodded yes – right on cue.

Olive made angry-sounding pig noises from underneath the window. She scratched on the wood siding of the schoolhouse just in case Mr. Bellows got brave and tried to have a look.

Mr. Bellows jumped back a few feet. "What in God's name is making that noise?"

Brittany moved to get a better look out the window.

Nina stood up to block the view from Brittany and Mr. Bellows. "That's Room 207's other pig, sir. Famous for being the world's second-fastest potbelly. He's very friendly except when he's cutting new teeth, like today."

"No wonder I'm getting calls. *Pigsty* this. And *Pigsty* that!" Mr. Bellows backed up even further. He bumped into Juliet's desk.

"It's just a nickname for our classroom," Juliet told him. "The other kids gave it to us. They're jealous because our pet pigs make us unique. It'd be hard to *win* a *Best Classroom* contest without being *unique.*"

"Or passing the *inspection*," Brittany announced sweetly. She pulled a crumpled pink memo paper from her pink sock and pitched it at Juliet.

```
Surprise classroom inspection tomorrow.
        Be ready or be disqualified.
```

"But this is dated *yesterday*!"

"I couldn't deliver it yesterday. I had more important things to do." Brittany Madison Heather Wales checked her manicure. "Besides, it says *surprise.*"

"SURPRISE!" Miles grabbed the lid of his desk and threw it open. The rest of Room 207 followed his lead and proudly displayed the insides of their desks.

The principal's eyebrows shot up. "Impressive," he admitted.

Brittany looked disgusted at the clean desks. She

tugged at Mr. Bellows. "Daddy asked me where I wanted the pool."

"Yes of course." He patted her on the head. "But I still must speak to Miss Chimney about this pigsty business. Then we can finally tear this place down."

Brittany Madison Heather Wales smiled. She tossed her head from side to side. She flung bouncy brunette hair everywhere. Finally she stopped flinging, pulled out something sparkly from the back of her skirt and put on the 'queen-for-a-day' tiara she'd been wearing all week. "My father will announce his sponsorship of the demolition at the pre-assembly in the auditorium tomorrow."

"*Pre-assembly*?" Miles asked.

"In the auditorium?" Adam asked.

"Tomorrow?" Todd asked.

They could almost taste the trouble they were in. That is until the wind changed direction. It blew a perfect poo-perfumed gust through the window and into the faces of Mr. Bellows and Brittany. They started choking and gagging. Juliet handed Brittany Butterbum's clean-up rag. Nina gave Mr. Bellows a box of Kleenex.

"Tell Miss Chimney I shall speak to her later. Preferably in the school staffroom," Mr. Bellows held a wad of tissue to his face and marched off.

The queen-for-a-day followed, staggering not-so-royally behind.

"Now that the pain-in-the-princess is gone . . ." Olive had popped up and stuck her head through the window, ". . . who wants to see Erik in a bra and heels?"

Erik hit Olive in the back of the head with a peach pit from the manure pile.

"I just want Miss Chimney back." Nina placed Butterbum on the teacher's desk.

Olive rubbed the goose egg hatching on her head. "We can't go to an assembly without her."

"On the contrary," said Rodan, "this opportunity may help us to find her."

"This should be good." Erik smirked.

"Shut up and let him finish," said Olive.

Rodan ignored them. "It would be too suspicious for all of us to enter the school . . ." he stopped mid-sentence, lifted his head, and stared into space.

"Space cadet central." Erik pointed at Rodan.

"Rodan? Enter the school and what?" Miles prompted.

Rodan came back to earth, ". . . to find clues to the mystery."

"WHAT MYSTERY!" Everyone was losing patience.

Rodan focused on them and smiled. "The mystery of the missing Miss Chimney."

"Hola! We have another puzzling puzzle," José called from the cloakroom. He poked his head around the wall. "Why is the pussy gato crying his little pussy eyes out?"

CRASH TEST

Amadeus had cried smoky tears till he was completely fogged in. No one could get a word out of him. Todd even offered him his emergency can of snack sardines.

The students of Room 207 headed home with shoulders slumped. They didn't talk about what had happened. They spit on their hands and swore they wouldn't tell anyone.

Samantha didn't consider her dog just anyone, so she told him. She lifted up one of his foot-long ears. "Puddin, I have something very important to tell you and you can't tell anyone . . . Miss Chimney is gone, Pourquoi too, and there is a *pre*-assembly tomorrow, probably to rehearse for the award ceremony for the Best Classroom Contest." Samantha sighed. "Which we definitely won't win because how are you supposed win without a teacher?" But Puddin didn't hear. He was fast asleep on her bed, where he wasn't supposed to be.

Exhausted from her day, Samantha curled up next to Puddin, started snoring, and didn't get up till the next morning.

Samantha was hungry because she had missed dinner last night. "Bet you'd kiss a cat for a bowl of Crunchy Pops." She nuzzled Puddin. Then she looked at her alarm clock – the one she had forgotten to set.

Big red numbers beamed 8:37 AM. "No . . . NOOOO!" she yelled.

Mrs. Napps ran into her room. "Sammy! Sammy-kins? Are you all right?"

"No Mom, I'm going to be late. *AGAIN*." Samantha sniffed the T-shirt she had slept in and decided it was good enough to wear to school. She grabbed some jeans and ran past her mom to the bathroom.

"I'll drive you. I want to see Miss Chimney anyway. I was in line at Moonie's Coffee House and I heard that Maynard Merdoc was told by Mrs. Hagen that Mrs. Erikson's son said your classroom was a pigsty." Mrs. Napps headed downstairs for her coat and car keys.

Samantha froze. "Ahh . . . you know what Mom? Erik's just being a jerk. He wants to change rooms 'cause

Miss Chimney gives him homework. All the other teachers were too afraid."

"Then I'd like to congratulate her on her bravery," Mrs. Napps said and smiled.

"You can't," Samantha stalled. "We have an assembly and Miss Chimney won't have time to talk to you this morning. I gotta hurry, Mom, or I'll miss it." Samantha slammed the bathroom door. She opened it quickly. "Sorry about the slamming." She shut the door and opened it again. "Can you make me a bagel and peanut butter? Thanks." She closed the door and locked it. Her heart pounded. Adrenaline raced through her veins so she had no problem shifting herself into high gear. Before the toilet had finished flushing her teeth were brushed, her hair was wrangled into a ponytail, and she'd jumped into her jeans.

Samantha gave Puddin a kiss on the head and flew down the stairs three at a time, grabbed the breakfast her mom held out at arm's length, and ran right through the sliding screen door. "Sorry about the screen thing," she said over her shoulder and ran all the way to school.

Everyone was waiting in the staff parking lot for Miles to arrive in the school bus. They cleared a path as Samantha came in for a landing.

Even Erik. He pointed at her and laughed. "Your fly is open."

Samantha went to kick him, but Erik moved and Samantha spun to the pavement.

"You okay?" Nina asked. She leaned down and whispered, "You're still flying low."

Samantha zipped up but stayed lying down. "I'm so tired I think I'll just sleep through the assembly here."

"Better get up or you'll be sleeping permanently." Olive yanked Samantha to her feet.

They heard the squealing tires three blocks away. It had to be Billy, the Safe Arrival Bus Company's worst driver, but nicest guy.

Todd cupped his hand around his ear to get a more accurate take on Billy's position. "Mulberry Street. He probably swerved to miss Jellybean." Jellybean was the dumbest cat this side of the equator. He always lounged in the middle of Mulberry and belonged to Mrs. North, the meanest lady in the neighborhood.

"I wish he'd run over Mrs. North," Adam said. "Yesterday she was on her porch and she hollered, 'I don't like you or your brother and neither does your grandmother!'"

Adam's imitation of Mrs. North was interrupted by screeching brakes, followed by the sound of metal being smashed and flattened two blocks away.

"Atwood Avenue!" Juliet was horrified. "I think I forgot to put the garbage can back in the garage."

They heard backing-up-school-bus beeps and the bus's big engine revving and backfiring like rifle shots. Then the bus hurtled down Pugwash Boulevard toward the parking lot.

Mr. Meyer had been walking his dogs up and down his driveway when the bus backfired. Now he was running in his slippers and bathrobe up Pugwash Boulevard. Well, he wasn't really running. He was being dragged at high speed by three barking, bus-crazed weiner dogs. They reached the entrance of the parking lot at the same time as the bus.

Billy figured the energetic man couldn't see his blinker, so he stuck his arm out the window and made a turning signal with his hand. The bus just missed Mr. Meyer because his dogs put on the brakes. The leash tightened and whipped him into the rose bushes. Mr. Meyer gave Billy a hand signal of his own that in some countries means "Do you want some coconuts?" but in this country is quite rude.

Billy didn't noticed. He was busy grinding down the gears to slow the bus. He threw open the doors and yelled at Miles, "I AIN'T GOT NO STOPPERS. LEFT MY BRAKES IN A GARBAGE CAN." Billy cranked the steering wheel to use a yellow dumpster as a crash pad but turned too late and only grazed it. "YOU'RE GONNA 'AVE TO JUMP."

Miles braced himself on the top step of the bus, aimed for the grass, and launched himself like a paratrooper. Without a parachute. He landed as hard as he would have if he'd fallen from the sky.

An older girl who looked like Miles leapt lightly off the bus.

Adam fell in love. He whistled. "Hey, Baby!"

Miles croaked to the others, "Oh-oh! That's my sister, Ruth."

Ruth strode over to a grinning Adam and hit him with a whopper. "You can call me Miss Marsbar."

Billy had rolled the bus out of the parking lot and was shifting gears before he noticed who was missing. "'ANG ON. WHERE'S THE LOVELY MISS CHIMNEY FOR OUR MORNING CHAT?" he yelled over the noise.

Everything but the bus became very still and very silent.

Juliet thought fast and cupped her hands around her mouth, "She forgot her mittens. She'll catch up at three."

"'ER DOG'S 'AVIN' KITTENS CAUSE 'ER CAT'S UP A TREE?"

"Umm . . . Yeesss," answered Juliet.

Olive started off for Room 207. "And that's nothin' compared to the cow Bellows is gonna have when he finds out Chimney is missing."

Nina nodded, then looked over her shoulder at Rodan. "Did you figure out how we're going to get her back?"

Rodan shook his head no.

Miles grabbed his arm. "If we can get you to the science lab would that help?"

"Maybe." Rodan, shrugged his shoulders.

They all walked quietly to class.

SCHOOL
OF RUTH

Ruth entered the schoolhouse and made a bee-line for the front of the room. She pulled a can of "New and Improved KILL-ALL" from her purse and started to spray Miss Chimney's desk.

José walked up to greet her. "Buenos dias!" he said. Then he sneezed right in Ruth's face.

Ruth went into shock.

José turned to the class and sighed. "Who is this flower and how did she come to my garden?"

"That's my older sister Ruth." Miles choked back the laughter. "She wants to work with kids."

"Does she like younger men?" José's eyes got all moony.

"Well she's pretty immature, but. . . ." Miles had to stop talking because Ruth shot him a look that would've stopped a charging rhino.

Ruth found her voice. "I'm nineteen, in second year at university." She walked José to his seat and planted him in it.

Rodan leaned over the back of his seat and whispered to Miles, "I wondered why Ruth was here. Pure brilliance to bring your sister. Did you tell her about Chimney?"

Ruth smacked a ruler on Rodan's desk. "No whispering! Got it?" She looked down her nose at him. "And for your information, Miles squealed the whole story. Cried on my pillow and everything. Begged me to come and pretend to be your teacher so you could get to the science lab and act out his little rescue mission." Ruth cackled and poked Miles in the ribs before leaving.

Miles winced. "She beat it out of me. Then threatened me with making me eat her cooking for a week and said I couldn't go to school unless she came too."

Olive was eavesdropping. "She into torture or something?"

"No." Miles sighed painfully. "She needs work experience to get her degree in Child Care."

Ruth stood at the front of the class and stared down at them. "I'm in charge. Got it?"

They nodded.

"I can't hear you."

"Yes, Miss Marsbar," they chanted in unison.

"Faster next time. Everybody to the school. NOW!" She charged to the old schoolhouse door, stopped, gave it a good sniff, wrinkled her face, then pried it open with her elbow.

The kids ran out underneath her armpit and headed for the school.

"Wait!" yelled Ruth. She marched to the front of the pack, knocking children aside as she went. "I go first. Got it?"

"Yes, Miss Marsbar!"

Miles had just picked himself up when Erik walked by and knocked him down again. "Smooth move bringing your sister, the *psycho*."

Ruth zoomed back into the middle of the pack and grabbed Erik by the T-shirt, "No talking. Got it?" She turned to her brother. "And you have detention for being a mess."

"Yes, Miss Marsbar," they said together.

"And no chewing gum or wiping your mouth or picking your nose with anything or sticking anything in your ear or touching cats or letting dogs lick you or walking in strange mud or singing or letting frogs jump on the back of your hand or putting your fingers in your hair or breathing funny or making one eye look one way while your other eye looks the other way or scratching or playing. . . ." Ruth recited her rules the whole way to the back entrance of the school.

Ruth stopped on the steps. She pulled a veil out of her purse.

Miles looked at his sister. "At least I talked her into wearing that."

"Good idea," said Rodan. "They won't know who she is."

"I didn't want her to scare the little kids either."

Ruth sprayed the push-bars of the steel doors and each one of her "students" as they went through the back entrance.

The halls were empty.

"Where is everyone?" Olive asked and they all looked at Rodan.

Rodan gave a nervous laugh. "How am I supposed to know?"

Ruth pinched Rodan to get his attention. "No laughing. Got it?"

Rodan nodded.

Ruth left his side to swoop in on her next target.

Rodan whispered to Miles, "I can't decide what your sister resembles more, an owl or a bat."

"I'll give you a clue," Miles replied. "She's not that smart."

CHICKEN OR BUNNY?

They tiptoed through the halls and up the stairs, freezing at the slightest sound. When they got to the science lab it was locked.

"Guess we'll have to break in," said Rodan.

"Cool." Erik was starting to think this rescue mission might be worth yesterday's embarrassment. He spit out his gum to see if it would stick to the doorknob.

Ruth arrived soundlessly at his side. "I said NO spitting. Got it?"

"Whatever." Erik was surprised to see her beside him.

Ruth leaned in but said in a loud voice, "If you're going to be a problem then maybe I should hold your hand?"

Everyone shrank as her voice bounced down the hall.

Erik winked at Ruth. In a flash she had grabbed Erik's hand and twisted his arm behind his back till they were holding hands between his shoulder blades.

Erik stood on his toes. "*Okay!*" he squeaked through clenched teeth.

Miles made a face. "I almost feel sorry for him. That's one of her favorite moves. Say "No" if she ever asks you to hold her hand," he said to Rodan.

"I couldn't possibly respond to your sister in a romantic way," Rodan whispered. "She scares me so much my brain cells freeze." He was serious.

Miles rubbed his eyebrow.

"No rubbing. Got it?" Ruth smacked at his hand.

"I'm trying to think how we're going to get through that door."

"For heaven's sake!" Ruth mugged Miles for his library card. She jiggled it between the door and the frame. The knob wouldn't turn. She tried a bobby pin in the keyhole. Still nothing. Her own house key, a curse, swearing, and a Tibetan chant still left them standing on the wrong side of the door. "This *always* works." Ruth opened her purse, pulled out a hammer and smashed the glass with one quick tap. She replaced the hammer, reached inside, and turned the knob.

Everyone stood welded to the floor.

Todd saw some green things that looked like pickles floating in a jar. "What are we waiting for?" He charged in.

Rodan scanned the room. "We need to find some test tubes and turn on the Bunsen burners."

Everyone but Erik fanned out to search. "What's a buns-and-burner?" he asked in Rodan's ear.

"Ahh . . .," Rodan stammered, a little shocked that Erik had spoken to him, ". . . it's a little cooker that gets liquid boiling in beakers."

Erik gave Rodan a blank look.

"In the movies scientists and bad guys use them a lot. It's got a *wicked* blue flame," Rodan explained.

"Cool." Erik smiled. "What are we going to do with it?"

Rodan thought the word "*we*" sounded strange coming from Erik. "Use it to analyze the slime and. . . ." Rodan's mouth fell open.

Miles turned up with a box of test tubes. "What's wrong with him?" He looked accusingly at Erik.

"Dunno. He just stopped talking."

Rodan swallowed hard. "I forgot to get a sample of the slime."

Miles dropped the box. Broken glass flew every-where.

Ruth didn't bother to yell at her brother. She was too

busy draping a stuffed fox around her shoulders, trying it on for size, thinking about her winter wardrobe.

Nina ran over to clean up. "Why don't you guys stop staring at each other and help me?"

"I'll help, Nina," Erik said, shoving glass under the display table with his foot. "You guys go back and I'll cover you." He was actually relieved that someone was doing something to bring back Miss Chimney. She had been helping him with his reading and homework after school – during his detentions – and even though she was a teacher, he secretly liked her. Plus he couldn't take much more of Ruth. She seemed more interested in hurting him than helping him.

Erik glanced at Ruth and shuddered.

"Ay, amigos!" José opened a steel door, "I think I find the cooking room."

Nina saw Erik's eyes light up. "Go. I got this."

Erik followed José through the door.

"Whooooaaa," they gasped.

The room looked like something out of *Frankenstein*. Plastic tubing hung from the ceiling, copper piping ran around the room, and shiny steel sinks were set into the counters. There were dozens of high tables with thick black slabs of marble. And on top were things that looked like candlestick holders with rubber hoses attached.

"Bunsen burners. Rodan said to turn them on." He worked up a gob of spit to loosen the valves.

Ruth was there in a second. "You spit and it'll be the last saliva you ever produce. Got it?"

Erik swallowed.

José winked at Ruth.

Ruth got José in a headlock and gave him a noogie with her knuckles.

"Ah my little passion fruit," José cooed, "I knew it. You are feeling the love too!"

It was Erik's laughter that brought the rest of 207 into the room.

Ruth dropped José and lunged for Erik.

Round and round the tables they went.

Between laughing and trying to escape Ruth, Erik was running out of breath.

Adam and Todd bet a week's worth of toilet cleaning on who would win.

Erik heard "toilet" and got an idea. "Wait a second," he held up his hand to stop the chase. "Anybody seen a can around here?"

"No making garbage." Ruth slowed to a halt. "Recycle everything."

"I don't think you want to recycle what I got to get rid of," Eric snickered.

Ruth put her hands on her hips. "Use your big-people words."

"He wants to skip to the loo," Todd said trying to be helpful.

"He wants to have a go in the dunny." Adam tried too.

Nina sighed. "He needs to use the little boys room."

"Well, that's your problem," Ruth snarked at Erik as she stomped away to try on more dead animals.

Nina took Erik's arm and led him out to the hallway. "The closest washrooms are the staff's." She pointed down the corridor. "They're on your left past the vending machine with toothpaste and coffee."

"Thanks," said Erik. "I'll pull the fire alarm if I see someone heading your way."

"Be careful." Nina slipped back inside the lab.

At first, Erik had just wanted to get away from Ruth, but now he really did have to go. The bathroom doors had been decorated for the harvest festival. One door had a picture of a bunny with a basket and someone had added fake fluff. On the other was a cartoon chicken. All the rest of the doors he'd walked past had numbers on them.

The bathroom doors had writing on them too, but since he couldn't read very well the writing didn't help. Erik was glad to see the chicken and bunny. He thought he could figure that out. "Now a chicken that lays eggs is a hen, and a hen is a female, so that must be the women's can," he said to himself and scratched his head. "And the bunny must be the Easter Bunny and he has to travel all the way around the world and jump over stuff and hide stuff where there are spiders and a girl couldn't do that so the Easter Bunny must be a male and this is the men's can." He pushed the door open and walked through.

The bathroom was all in pink. Pink sinks. Pink soap. Pink paper towel dispenser with pink paper towels. Even pink mouthwash. Erik didn't notice that everything was pink because he was color-blind. It all just looked gray to him. He did notice there were no urinals, and at least a dozen stalls. Normally he would go all the way to the end so he could bang on all the doors coming and going. He was getting desperate, though, so he chose the first one.

There was a rose in a vase on top of the toilet. There was a shaggy cover on the tank. There was a luxurious fluffy mat on the floor that wrapped around the bottom

of the toilet. And in the stall next door there was a pair of heels with a pair of feet in them.

"Hey!" Erik blurted, "this doesn't look like. . . ."

A woman shrieked.

The lights flashed and a siren wailed.

Mr. Bellows burst into the bathroom. "How did I know it was going to be *you*?" he yelled.

The alarm had practically bursted everyone's eardrums. Room 207's students abandoned the lab and made it out the back door seconds before Anna Swan Heights went into lockdown.

Mr. Bellows marched Erik to his office. He held Erik by the ear with one hand. With the other he grabbed the microphone for the PA. "I'm standing here with a cheater. A cheater who tried to break into staff quarters to find out who won Best Classroom before the official announcement. Therefore, the preassembly is canceled. The contest is now closed. And the real assembly with the representatives from Dream Creams will be moved up to this afternoon at 2:30. *There will be no more shenanigans!*"

After his 'visit' with the principal, Erik walked slowly back to the schoolhouse. He didn't tell his classmates he'd been suspended. He gave them the only news he thought they'd care about. "We're disqualified."

"Erik, you blew it!" Olive was mad.

"How was I supposed to know the chicken was a rooster and not a hen?" he said to the back of her head.

Olive turned and glared at him. "Can't you read a bathroom door?"

Erik didn't answer her. He just wished he wasn't the reason everyone looked angry or gloomy.

Ruth snapped her fingers. "Everyone line up in front of me. No butting in. Got it?"

Room 207's students looked at each other and nodded in silent agreement. Instead of making a straight line behind Ruth, they circled around her and made her the center of attention.

Olive put her hands on her hips. "We're sick of having you boss us around."

"Yeah. We don't need you anymore." Todd crossed his arms over his chest

"GOT IT?" Adam raised an eyebrow.

"Miles?" Ruth eyed her brother.

"Ah, thanks for coming?" Miles shrugged.

"Fine," said Ruth. She lifted her chin and squared her shoulders, "I'm sure they would appreciate my help in the kindergarten." She stomped off to Miss Weedwhacker's room.

When she got there, a little girl the other kids called Patty Potty-mouth, was drawing red spots on her face with a marker.

Ruth bent over and got right in Patty's face. "What are you doing?" she demanded.

Patty smiled. "Making chicken pocks!" she answered.

"Chicken pox is a childish disease. No making chicken pox. Got it?"

Patty frowned, "No. But my brother does."

HOW TO
SPELL LOSER

No one spoke as they ate their lunches at their desks. They felt abandoned. No Miss Chimney. No Pourquoi. No sign of Amadeus.

Nina went to Butterbum's drawer and lifted her out. She didn't even squeak when Nina touched her ticklish spot.

"She hasn't touched her carrots or had any water from her bowl," Nina said, starting to cry. "I miss her too," she whispered in Butterbum's little ear.

Rodan checked the garbage can. "Well, it doesn't appear that the slime has changed," he said. "I would assume that's a good thing, but I'm not an expert in slime."

Erik took a chocolate bonbon he'd stolen from the

staff bathroom out of his pocket. He unwrapped it and it fell on the floor.

He grabbed it as it rolled away. He checked the chocolate for hairs or stuff Pourquoi might have tracked in from the manure pile. It seemed okay to him. Erik looked up and caught Olive sneering at him. "What, Olive? It's the five-second rule. You can eat anything that falls on the ground if it's been down less than five seconds."

"You're such a loser," said Olive. "In case you don't know how to spell *loser* I'll tell you . . . it's E-R-I-K."

"Hey Olive," Miles piped up, "why don't you check out your entry in the dictionary? It's under B for B-U-L-L-Y."

Erik didn't feel like eating his bonbon anymore. He walked to the garbage, dropped the candy in, and headed for the door.

"*CHOCOLATE!*" The word erupted from the slime.

"Shut up, Olive!" Erik exploded.

Olive looked stunned. "It wasn't me." She stared at the can.

"*MORE CHOCOLATE!*"

Rodan was the first one there. "Amazing. Talking primordial ooze."

Nina pushed him aside. "Give us back Miss Chimney!" she yelled and kicked the can, "and *maybe* we'll give you more chocolate."

Amadeus materialized on Miss Chimney's desk and spooked Butterbum. "That's not what it wants." He put his paw on Butterbum's back.

Nina grabbed Butterbum, backed away, and tucked the guinea pig into her pocket.

Olive walked up to the teacher's desk and slapped her palms down. "How do you know what it wants?"

"I spoke to *it* last evening," he hissed at her.

Olive backed off and crossed her arms. "Why didn't you tell us this morning?"

"Because you are rude to me." Amadeus licked his paw. "It was absolute heaven to get a quiet night's sleep. The depressed pond hog didn't chatter and squeak all night and Pourquoi wasn't here to snore the pipes to the breaking point and the gas he...."

Miles interrupted. "What does the slime want?"

"What's in it for me?" Amadeus stopped preening himself.

Todd came forward. "I've still got tuna fish left from lunch."

"White or brown bread?"

"What's the difference?" Todd shook his head. "You can't eat it anyway."

"White or brown?" Amadeus repeated.

"White."

"I will assist you motley crew with your mission on one condition." Amadeus had their full attention. "You will not let my place of residence come to misfortune."

"Room 207 . . . is your *home* . . . that's why you were crying." Nina looked sad for him.

"More like my jail. But yes, that's why the ungentlemanly show of emotion," admitted Amadeus as he looked away. "Because you lot would just allow that horrible little witch to let her father knock it down."

Nina walked back to the desk and sidled up beside him. "Amadeus," she said trying to figure out how to stroke him, "you may be a pain in the bum . . . but we would never let anyone tear down this schoolhouse if it meant the end of you." Scratching the air under his chin made him purr.

"I should tell you that your educator-gulping gelatin blob heard me blubbering and told me his own sob story. He misses his family," Amadeus sighed and looked accusingly at Miles. "He says you kidnapped him when he was just a little slime ball."

OPERATION SLIME BUCKET

Samantha was more awake and alert than she had ever been in her life. "We need a plan. The best plan ever."

Everyone stared at Miles hopefully.

Miles panicked. His legs twitched. The door seemed a football field away.

Rodan saw Miles eyeing the door. He realized that Miles was facing the dread of letting them all down. Rodan had done an extra credit science paper called *The Fight or Flight Theory of Man* and he recognized the symptoms of pre-flight in Miles. He wanted to say something that would make Miles stay. "You're my best friend Miles," he began. "It would be understandable if you ran away. But I think you should stay because I know you can do this." Rodan smiled.

Rodan's confidence spurred Miles' brain into action.

"Okay, we've got to get the slime back to our old room, right?"

"Right!"

Miles turned to Rodan. "How heavy do you think the slime plus the garbage can is?"

Rodan walked over quickly, grabbed the handles and tried to move the can. "My estimate is about two hundred pounds."

"We can't drag that lot back to the school." Adam looked defeated.

"No we can't," Miles agreed. "And even if we could, we'd have to do it without being seen."

Erik had an idea, but he didn't know if the others trusted him or even wanted his help. What had Miss Chimney said to him about making friends? *You can't win if you don't bet some chips.* He raised his hand and felt like he was going to lose his cookies.

Miles hesitated. "Yes, Erik?"

"You know the janitor . . . Mr. Drum?"

Miles nodded yes.

Erik took a deep breath and played all his chips before they could say his idea was stupid and he lost his nerve. "He's got that little tractor cart thing he uses to haul stuff like garden hoses and tables for track-and-field day and he puts the trash cans from the playground in it and takes them to the dumpster parked at the side of the maintenance shed and we could use the cart to take the slime bucket to the service elevator and put it on a dolly to wheel it to Miss Chimney's old Room 207 . . ." He ran out of breath.

Miles didn't hesitate this time. "Can you take care of that?"

"Yep." Erik grinned.

"What about keys?"

"No problem." Erik shuffled his feet. "I can hot-wire it."

Everyone looked at him suspiciously.

Erik turned a bright shade of pink that Brittany Madison Heather Wales would have said was "so last year." He looked away from their accusing eyes and mumbled, "My mom's a mechanic for the circus. . . ."

"Oi!" Todd yelped, ". . . the ol' Seal Breath Circus?"

Erik kept his eyes on the floor and nodded.

"Our mum works there too!" Todd punched Erik's arm. "Your mum's helped our mum loads of times. She says the monkeys are real roughies, always pinching the keys to the trucks. And Dad's always losing the ones for his clown car. They told us the mechanic helped them out, but we didn't know that was your mum."

Todd and Adam grabbed Erik by the arms and pulled him out the door. "We'll just help him juice the trolley," Adam yelled over his shoulder. "Back in five shakes of a wombat's tail."

"Wombats don't have tails," said Todd.

"Whatever, we're going to nick a truck to save a nice duck and a fat pig and it's loads more interesting than maths!"

Erik didn't understand a word of what they were saying. And the only time he was hauled by the arm was when he was being dragged to the principal's office or clothes shopping with his mom, but this time Erik was happy to go along for the ride. He hoped he'd see Miss Chimney again so he could tell her he followed her advice and came out a winner.

Miles paced around Miss Chimney's desk and made Butterbum dizzy. "Okay, we have a way to get the slime back to its family. Now we've got to make sure we don't

get caught." He rubbed his temples. "Who would be most likely to catch us?"

"Blueberry Bellows," Nina whispered.

"Nurse Payne." Juliet shuddered.

"Mr. Drum," Pugh added.

"Exactly . . . those three." Miles stopped pacing. "I need you guys to keep them occupied." He grinned. "Here's how."

Miles got a big piece of yellow construction paper from the supply cupboard and some markers from the art shelf. He drew a rough sketch of the front hall by the office. "Nina, this is you." He held up a blue marker. "Can you barge into the principal's office and start bawling your eyes out? You could get an onion out of the garden or think of something really sad."

Nina nodded. Tears flooded her eyes. "Miss Chimney and Pourquoi are being held hostage by the slime and Butterbum's on a hunger strike because she misses them so much," she bawled.

Miles passed Nina a box of tissue, then turned to Juliet. "Juliet, this is you." He uncapped the red marker and drew a little stick figure running. "Run down to Nurse Payne's office and tell her that Pugh is really sick. Say he has the plague or he's covered in dust. And then don't let her out of your sight."

"Okay," agreed Juliet, "but you owe me one."

"Maybe ... but I don't think you'll want to trade jobs with Rodan." Miles drew an orange circle around the spot in the school garden where Professor Shrimpington was buried. "I'm sorry, buddy, but you're the one who's used to dissecting dead stuff."

"Just tell me what my mission is," Rodan said solemnly.

"Dig up the Professor. He'll be nice and gooey by now."

Pugh turned green.

Miles smiled. "Pugh, you're going to stand outside

the office and throw up when Rodan shows you what's left of the Professor."

"Rodan, you run into the office and tell Mrs. Watson that Pugh puked. She'll call Mr. Drum on the PA for a cleanup."

Miles pointed to where the service elevator was on the ground floor. "José, can you see my drawing alright?"

"Si."

"Go to this elevator and make sure it's waiting for us. You're new at the school, so if anyone asks what you're doing there just tell them you're lost. Okay?"

"Yes, YES, YES, El Capitan!" José saluted. "The elevator, she will be waiting for you with open doors." He ran off toward the school.

"What about me?" Olive was afraid she'd be left out.

"You can drive the tractor thing when the criminals get back," Miles said. "Samantha can stay here and tell anybody who comes looking for us that she missed the assembly, but the rest of us are there."

"That's a good plan," declared Rodan.

"Except," asked Miles, "what time is it?"

"2:17." Rodan knew what Miles was thinking. "Afternoon recess just finished."

"Right." Miles clapped his hands. "We've got thirteen minutes to pull off Operation Slime Bucket."

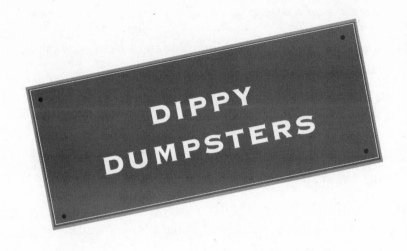

DIPPY DUMPSTERS

R odan met them at the elevator doors on the second floor.

"Well?" Miles asked him.

"Decomposition of an organism...."

"Pugh puked on cue?"

"Precisely."

"Comin' through," Erik warned and hung on to the dolly with all his strength as he wheeled the slime bucket out of the elevator. He stopped just outside the doors.

Everyone listened for any light-switch flicking, yelling, door slamming, red-pen scratching, coffee-sipping, or other sounds that teachers make.

"Okay," Miles directed, "let's surround Erik. If any-body comes, stand in front and act natural."

Olive looked at Erik. "I can say I caught you in the girls' bathroom and I'm taking you to the office."

Erik turned candy-apple red.

"Sorry, Erik . . . I didn't mean. . . ." Olive looked directly into his eyes and apologized.

"It's okay. It's a good cover." Erik had never noticed her eyes before.

"Listen my peachy lovebirds," said Todd, "we've got to get Slimy here back to his family before the bell rings."

Everyone fell in and they crept down the hall.

They stopped in front of the door with a new steel plate that said ROOM 207.

"Oh no!" Olive gasped.

The wall between their classroom and the hall had been repaired. The caution tape had been taken off the door.

Rodan's hand shook as he reached for the door. "*Maybe. . . .*"

They all jumped back when the door opened from the inside.

"You kids have perfect timing." A man wearing a construction hat and a name tag with Albert written on it stood in the open doorway. "Wanna come in and check out your *new and improved* classroom?"

They stuck their heads inside the room.

New walls. New windows. New desks. Even Sheldon the skeleton had been replaced by a mannequin with zip-off skin and squishy rubber life-size organs.

There was no slime anywhere.

Miles almost choked.

Adam and Todd didn't laugh, and they usually laughed at everything.

Erik wanted to cry.

Rodan recovered first. "We should return to our fellow students and pack our belongings," he said to Albert and turned away.

"Send Miss Chimney on ahead." Albert slapped Rodan on the back. "I can't wait to see your teacher's face."

"Us too," Miles said and kept Rodan from going head first into the slime bucket.

They walked backwards and waved to Albert till he

went back inside their new old room. They got back in the service elevator and pushed the button for the boiler room.

"Now what?" asked Erik.

Miles shrugged. "I got nothin.'"

Rodan held up his finger. "This is a setback, but let's look at this logically." He pushed the STOP button. "They had to put the ruined contents of the classroom somewhere."

"The dippy dumpsters!" exclaimed Todd.

"It's Friday." Erik looked discouraged.

"Duh!" Olive felt that she had been nice to Erik for nothing.

"Duh," he said back. "They *empty* the dumpsters on Friday mornings."

"The green ones by Mr. Drum's shed where we nicked the buggy?" Todd asked.

"Yeah, those are the ones."

"Well what about the yellow one with the graffiti in the staff parking lot?" Everyone stared at Adam. "The one Billy's been using as a bus stop. It had little black triangles on it."

Rodan hit the START button with his fist. "That's not graffiti. It's a toxic waste symbol. *That* must be where they put the wreckage from 207."

José was waiting for them at the bottom. He saw right away that things hadn't gone as planned. "Nobody, they come by. But Nicest Teacher, she come back?"

"Not yet, but we have another plan," Miles told him.

José smiled. "Mi padre he says if a cucaracha he get in your taco, then you make another one."

"Your dad's a smart guy . . . okay, you go help with the second taco and I'll go make sure there'll be no more cucarachas-cock-a-roaches." Miles headed for the office.

Erik started Mr. Drum's cart without keys again. Olive backed it up. Rodan made a ramp from a broken desktop and leaned it against the bumper. Adam and Todd dragged the can up the ramp and into the back of the cart. José whistled and kept a lookout.

Olive turned around in the driver's seat, "Can you guys make any more noise?"

Todd made faces at her and blew raspberries.

Everyone jumped on the cart and Olive threw the stick shift into gear. The engine revved but the cart didn't move.

"The slime has gotten heavier," said Rodan.

José stuck his head over the side of the cart. "And the tire, she is as flat as a tortilla." He pointed to the right rear tire.

They were so pumped up from the excitement they hadn't noticed.

"We're in the poo now." Todd was stumped.

"Shaving cream!" exclaimed Erik.

"What are you talking about?"

"Old circus trick." Erik grinned. "You fill the tire with shaving cream."

Olive's eyes were the only thing she could get rolling.

"That'll work, anything with mass will fill it up," Rodan agreed, "and the cans are pressurized." He looked at his watch. "We've only got five minutes before the bell."

Erik winked. "I'll be back in two."

Olive drove like a madwoman across the playground.

The boys hung on for their lives.

Like a pack of wild dogs Pugh, Juliet, Nina, and Miles ran across the parking lot to meet them at the dumpster.

"Put it in reverse," said Erik, "then we'll all have to lift the can."

Olive did as Erik ordered and everyone climbed on board and grabbed the can, which now seemed to weigh a ton.

Pugh climbed on top of the dumpster, plugged his nose, and lifted the lid.

"On three," Miles directed. "One . . . two. . . ."

BANG!

The tires blew. Shaving cream flew everywhere. The slime almost slopped over the side of the cart.

"THREE!" yelled Miles.

They shoved the can, slime and all, into the dumpster. Pugh dropped the lid and threw himself on top of it.

They didn't dare breathe.

The dumpster started to vibrate. Then it rocked. Then it jumped around and its wheels left the ground. Pugh looked like he was on a bucking bronco.

Then the dumpster stopped moving.

Slurping sounds echoed inside the bin.

"Pourquoi, it's so dark in here." Miss Chimney's voice sounded hollow. "I can't see you, pig, but I can hear you slurping. Stop that! You don't know where it's been."

Nina stepped forward and knocked softly on the side of the dumpster, "Hello?"

"Nina? Is that you?"

"We're all here . . . is all of you in there?" asked Nina.

"Why don't you open this lid and we'll check."

Miles and Erik each took a corner. The heavy metal

lid was stuck for a moment and then gave way. Pourquoi came flying out. He jumped on Nina, knocked her down, and licked her face.

Miss Chimney popped up like a jack-in-the-box. "How lovely to see you all. Do you have any more chocolate?"

"I gave you my last piece," said Erik as he helped her over the side and onto the parking lot.

"That was very thoughtful . . ." Miss Chimney put her arm around him, ". . . and it was very kind of you all to rescue me," she told the rest of her students.

They rushed forward and put their arms around her. Then they all started talking at once.

"Miles came up with this brilliant plan. . . ."

"Because Billy crashed the bus. . . ."

"Erik stole Mr. Drum's cart and Mr. Bellows' shaving cream . . ."

"The Professor doesn't look so good. . . ."

"All over the glass wall of the office. . . ."

"Butterbum missed you. . . ."

"Don't give Olive your car. . . ."

Mrs. Chimney held up her hands for them to stop yelling all at once. "Your adventure sounds a lot more exciting than mine. I should say good-bye to Simon and then you can tell me all about it." She untangled herself from the web of children.

Mrs. Chimney opened the lid to the dumpster and they all looked inside.

The slime was bubbling and sloshing and swirling a million different colors.

Todd stared in amazement. "Looks like they're having a real kick-on."

Miss Chimney laughed. "If you mean a family reunion party I think you're right." She cupped a hand around her mouth and whispered, "Good-bye, Simon. I think you'll enjoy your new home at the dump." Miss Chimney lowered the lid gently.

"Where did it come from?" asked Rodan.

"Miss Weedwhacker's kindergarten." Miss Chimney started for the old schoolhouse.

"Those cookie crumblers!" Adam shook his head.

The bell rang.

Miss Chimney stopped in her tracks and checked her watch. "School's not over yet . . . what's that bell for?" she asked. "Assembly?"

"To announce the winners of the stupid contest," Olive grumbled.

Everyone's face fell like they'd dropped their ice-cream cones on the sidewalk.

Miss Chimney straightened her dress. She smoothed out her bangs. She cleared slime from her sinuses. "*We're late*," she announced and started for the school.

Miles caught her arm. He adjusted his glasses, "Actually, we're disqualified."

"Pourquoi?"

The potbelly snorted loudly at the sound of his name and nudged Miles. "Long story. We got caught breaking into the school to rescue you."

"Even more reason to hurry," declared Miss Chimney.

Room 207 sprinted for the school.

Nina ran to get Butterbum.

Erik stayed behind to walk with Miss Chimney and fill her in.

"You've all had a rough time." She patted Erik on the shoulder. "Come on, Pourquoi." She pulled the pig by the ear. "One more adventure then we bubble bath and double-chocolate."

At the mention of chocolate Erik's throat tightened up. He squeezed a question out. "Did you know the Easter Bunny is a girl?"

"Yes, I read about it in a book." Miss Chimney shot him a questioning look.

Erik swallowed hard, "I could use some help with my reading."

Pourquoi thought Erik said *eating* and rubbed up against his leg.

AT LAST

When Room 207 reached the auditorium Miss Chimney yelled, "Forget single file!" They stormed the double doors together.

The place sounded like a turkey barn right before Thanksgiving.

Without breaking stride, Miss Chimney put two fingers in her mouth and let go the loudest whistle in the history of the auditorium. The piercing sound she made was one thing, but it was the way she looked that stopped everyone's chatter. As Miss Chimney sailed down the aisle she left slime slobber, bits of old carpeting, crumbly drywall, and a trail of TV cameramen in her wake.

Brittany Madison Heather Wales looked up from where she was sitting, stage left, in a tall swivel-chair having her hair and make-up done. Above her head microphones dangled from booms and tangles of wires hung like spider webs. Miles thought he saw some wires move as if they had caught an invisible lunch.

At stage right Bellows was talking to his niece, Miss Weedwhacker, and Mr. Wales. They looked surprised to see Miss Chimney and downright shocked to see her climb the steps of the stage and walk right past them.

"May I have everyone's attention please?" she asked, even though she already had it. "I've come to make a case for Room 207's re-entry into the contest. They entertained, educated, and earned the most contest points at the Harvest Festival . . ."

There were a lot of laughs and one boo from Mark Woolly.

". . . they passed the classroom inspection given without warning, *Brittany.*" She shot Brittany a look.

The auditorium fell silent.

"Are you addressing *me?*" Brittany glared back at Miss Chimney and waved the make-up and hair guy away. She whipped out her cell phone and called her father on his cell. "Daddy! Pick-up now!" she yelled and threw a hairbrush at him.

Miss Chimney blew her stack. "Young lady, will you please shut your trap!" All the staff and most of the school cheered. Brittany Madison Heather Wales dropped her phone and her mouth fell open.

Amadeus materialized on her lap and stuffed a moth-eaten mouse into her yap. He dusted off his paws, leapt to the floor, and sent her swivel chair for a high-speed spin. He picked up her phone, called 'the other side,' and made a reservation. "Thank you," he said into the phone. Then he addressed Miss Chimney. "The kindness of your pupils," he winked at Nina, "has set me free, but I should very much like to stay and see how this saga ends."

"How wonderful for you," Miss Chimney said softly as she dabbed at a tear with her dirty sleeve, "but I will miss your music."

The audience couldn't believe their ears and eyes. Mr. Wales was rooted to the floor.

Miss Chimney motioned for Room 207 to join her on stage. "To continue," she began, "as far as working together, that's what they were doing very well until the unfortunate incident in the Ladies Room."

Several girls giggled. Even Erik laughed.

Miss Chimney smiled. "You see, they were trying to help me out of a very messy situation and they had to do it on their own as I was consumed by the problem."

Mr. Bellows started toward her. "Now, I don't see how any of this. . . ."

Amadeus launched himself at the principal and roared like a lion.

Miss Chimney carried on. "They have outdone themselves in all three categories of the contest. I wouldn't be here without them." She took a couple steps back and gently pushed forward Miles and Rodan, Samantha and Juliet, Pugh and José, Olive and Erik, Nina and Butterbum, Todd and Adam. "That's why Room 207 is the *best* classroom."

Only the creaking of a folding seat folding could be heard.

"*AND*. . . THEY WILL SHARE THEIR ICE CREAM WITH YOU!"

"Oi! Yelled Todd.